CARING FOR CATHY

CARING
FOR
CATHY

GIL HOGG

Matador
9 De Montfort Mews
Leicester LE1 7FW, UK
Tel: (+44) 116 255 9311 / 9312
Email: books@troubador.co.uk
Web: www.troubador.co.uk/matador

ISBN 978 1906221 478

Typeset in 12.5pt Bembo by Troubador Publishing Ltd, Leicester, UK
Printed in the UK by The Cromwell Press Ltd, Trowbridge, Wilts, UK

Matador is an imprint of Troubador Publishing Ltd

To Angie

1

The dog was there when David came downstairs for breakfast, a golden Labrador, barking wildly on the porch outside the main doors. The animal pawed the glass panes as though it wanted to break through. Several residents were beginning to gather curiously in the lobby, quite safe, because the glass was thick, and the doors were kept locked at all times. David had to pause for a few moments, to make sure that he understood what was happening.

The dog wasn't angry, he decided; it was agitated, jumping about excitedly, and chasing its tail. And it had its attention on Cathy, in her wheelchair, well to the front of the other watchers. Cathy herself was excited. She was shouting, and waving her arms.

David pushed past the other residents, and went to her. He bent over, and put his head close to hers.

"Is it your dog?" he asked.

He knew that Cathy owned a dog. Her husband used to bring the dog on visits, but had given up months ago because he said it was a nuisance.

Cathy nodded, and made a sound which indicated yes, "Mmmmh!"

Rose appeared, and placed her wide frame protectively in front of the audience, her back to the doors and windows.

"All right now, everybody, in to breakfast. It's breakfast time. Don't keep cook waiting. Go along. The dog won't hurt you. I'll get somebody to take it away," she said.

Rose seemed not to notice that far from being alarmed, the exuberance of the animal had set smiles on the faces of the residents. One or two were joking, and trying to attract the dog's attention.

David tried to tell Rose it was Cathy's dog. He pointed at Cathy, and opened his mouth, but no words came. This sometimes happened when he wanted words urgently. Rose looked questioningly at him through her thick lenses.

"Come on now, David, follow me."

She swayed on her thick, veiny legs, wheeling Cathy behind the crowd, toward the dining room. Rose was very old for a nurse, but with most of her lumpy body hidden in a loose blue uniform, all you noticed was her energy, and the slate coloured eyes, swimming under her spectacles.

Cathy had a place for her wheelchair at a table with David, and Mark Demeter, but it wasn't possible for David to speak to Cathy about the dog in the dining room. Dishes and cutlery clattered. The residents were all chattering. The care assistants were talking above this noise, as they served the food. Mark, dressed this morning in a grey suit, with a white shirt, and a green bow tie, was speaking loudly. He was addressing the occupants of an adjoining table, but they weren't listening. Cathy made an anguished sound that came from deep inside her, but wasn't a shout or a scream.

"Arrrrrgh, arrrrgh, arrrrgh!"

Her arm swept across the tray mounted on her wheelchair. The plastic plate of oatmeal porridge, unfortunately placed there, and waiting to be fed to her by a carer, was splashed on the floor. Having somebody push their food on to the floor was a commonplace event, and the staff would clean up without any recriminations. What struck David was that Cathy was disturbed by the arrival of the dog.

After finishing his cereal, David left the dining room. He would have to wait to see Cathy. The dog had gone from the porch. He went into the deserted sitting room, seated himself at the upright piano with the front panels missing, and began to tinker with a few bars. A fragment, of Liszt – he thought it was Liszt – came to him, before he went on to the only two tunes he could remember at that moment, *It's a Long Way To Tipperary* and *Yes, Sir, That's My Baby*.

It would take a while for a care assistant to feed Cathy with a spoon. She was usually one of the last to finish eating. Then she had to be taken to the toilet, which required two helpers. After that, she usually had a cigarette. This had to be held to her lips, in the smoking room, by a carer. Cathy had explained to David that she had Huntington's, a genetic disease. A bad seed in her family had sprouted, by surprise, in her. To David, her mind seemed intact, while many of her other bodily functions had failed, or were failing.

Cathy had arrived at Denby Hall within days of David's arrival, about three years ago, and they had always been friendly. She had been much more capable then. She could converse, and walk unaided for a few yards. She could feed herself. She had impressed David as a dignified person, with her long thin neck, her copious head of dark hair, and her smooth, small-featured face. She was full of jokes and laughter, despite her affliction. Cathy was a youthful-looking fifty then, more than twice his age. They used to sing, and play music on the guitar and piano in those early days, and Cathy had introduced David to her visiting husband, Desmond, as 'My special friend.'

David had a dim memory of getting off the bus, on the tree-lined country road near his father's house in Somerset, when he was twenty. The day had been washed into bright colours by a spring shower. Above was a rag of blue sky. The rain was dripping from the leaves of the oak trees which lined the road, and the tarmac glistened. The box hedges on the far side of the road, which hid the house, were smoothly clipped. The grass verge was mown like a bowling green. He was home from the Royal College of Music for a long weekend.

In just a second, as David slung his pack over his shoulder, and hurriedly stepped out from behind the noisy engine of the bus, to cross the road, the life he lived then, ended. The end was the terrifying snarl of an animal of red painted metal and chrome, leaping at him; then nothing. No sensation of pain. He was told much later that the car wasn't even speeding.

What started then, was a long slow ascent from darkness, through mist that had never entirely cleared, and still hung in wisps around David's judgement. As Cathy had explained her life to him, from the perspective of her cell, as she called it – the place inside her head where her brain was – he had tried to plot the mental map of his own new life on a largely empty canvas. David had no recollection of childhood, of school, or the music academy. A lot of the things he had been taught, like English, elementary mathematics and geography, remained imperfectly. But he had no memory of who taught him, or where. He could remember some songs and music, and he retained a small measure of skill with the piano. His hands at least escaped serious injury; almost the only part of him that did.

David's physical problems were manageable. It was his state of mind which troubled his father, and Caroline Higgins, his psychotherapist. He realised that he was a worry and, to please them, he had sometimes pretended to have memories and interests, like following Manchester United, or gardening, which really he did not have. But he had also recognised that he could not go on pretending just to please. In any event, his father and Caroline were perceptive, and would eventually see through him.

David had cooperated as far as he could in his sessions with Caroline at Denby Hall. She probed into the fog in his head very gently. These meetings were designed to bring him back to the world he had left. He felt he was standing on one side of a chasm, reaching across to Caroline, and she to him, but without success. At times the mist cleared, and their fingertips could almost touch. At other times, the fog between them was impenetrable. And there were occasions when he had a clear view, but still the space between them was as wide and deep as the Grand Canyon. David imagined that Cathy, of course, was on his side of the chasm, along with most of the Denby Hall inmates. They all looked across the canyon, all of them marooned.

More than three quarters of an hour elapsed before David was able to intercept Cathy's carer outside the smoking room.

"I'll take her for a while, Doreen," he said, and pushed Cathy's wheelchair out of the fug, into the sitting room. It was an accepted exchange, and Cathy made no sign, except a slight facial expression of agreement.

David sat on a stool by the wheelchair, and leaned close to Cathy. He had found that although Cathy could not converse in ordinary tones, or speak words clearly, if he whispered faintly to her, she could sometimes breathe an understandable reply. The doctor, nurses, and other staff, did not always appreciate the usefulness of this method. And David had also gained the ability, over the years that he had known Cathy, to interpret, to a degree, the babbles and moans to which her speech had been reduced.

"Is that dog... Polly?" he asked, trying to remember the name of Cathy's dog.

"Mmmmh. Poppy."

"Yes, Poppy. I remember. How did she get here?"

He could not work out Cathy's reply, and decided it was an unnecessary question. What was important was that the dog was here, and Cathy was pleased to see it, but obviously upset at the implications of its arrival.

David had been buoyed up by the feverish pleasure of the animal as it capered on the porch. Relatively few patients had visitors, and those who came, did not come frequently. Denby Hall was a place that friends and loved ones at home were tacitly reluctant to visit. This was not necessarily because they were unfeeling, or because Denby Hall was forbidding – it was not. The Hall was a place that was unsettling to people outside. To David, Poppy's arrival was so affecting because it was an enthusiastic acceptance of the place – admittedly by an animal – an acceptance that seemed to flower, and include those who had witnessed it.

"I'm going to try to find out what's happened to Poppy since she disappeared from the porch," he said, in a low voice to Cathy.

Cathy breathed a sound that was "Yes." David left her with a helper, and found Rose in the dispensary. He stood by the door hesitantly. Rose could be sharp.

"What do you want, David? I'm busy."

He watched Rose, her fingers in rubber gloves, selecting various colours and sizes of pills from a cupboard, and arranging them in slots on a tray. She was studying a chart on the wall at the same time, preparing the lunchtime doses. The names of all the residents were written on the chart, and against the slots on the tray. David had pain-killers. Cathy had Olanzapine to control spasmodic movement.

"The … dog?"

"Now, don't distract me, David. I have to get this right."

Rose was a nurse of an old-fashioned kind, which Cathy, in the time when she could speak fluently, had described as 'The Rub & Scrub School of Nursing'. She had a stern eye, but a soft underbelly.

It was easier for David to talk while Rose was concentrating on the pills.

"I aah… w-wondered about the dog."

"It's tied up outside. Keith is going to get somebody to take it to the pound later."

Keith was in charge of the day shift. The pound, and the town's dogs' home and kennels were about a mile down the road.

"Why are you asking?" Rose said, covering the tray with cellophane, setting it on a side table, and swinging round to fix David in the frames of her spectacles. Her nose and cheeks were randomly placed lumps of dough. Her eyes looked like raw oysters in their shells.

"It's … Cathy's dog."

"Well, she can't keep it here. Now that's obvious, David, isn't it? She can't look after it herself, and this is a home for sick people. We can't have dogs roaming around licking germs all over things, and biting, can we?"

"I could… look after Poppy, in the garden outside the Hall."

"No you couldn't. You're not well enough."

"I could take Poppy back to the pound."

"No, David, you couldn't. It'll be a business handing the dog over. You can't just walk in there, and walk out. You couldn't do it."

"Come on, Rose … I'm n-not that useless."

"What you really want to do is to get hold of the dog, isn't it?"

Rose had a faint look of self-satisfaction about her mind-reading powers, honed over forty years on people like him.

"I … g-guess so."

"Well, you can't have it. And who told you the dog was Cathy's?"

"She did."

Rose clamped her lips sceptically. "I expect her husband didn't tie it up at home, and it escaped. It'll have to go back. Keith's found it, and he'll sort it later."

After this rebuff from Rose, David went to his room. He assumed that Keith had not yet had time to make an arrangement to remove Poppy, and therefore that she would still be tied up outside.

David's room was on the second floor facing south, overlooking the sparse trees in the Denby Hall grounds. The empty sea of the English Channel filled the windows with a grey brightness, like mercury, which merged into the sky. He put on a padded anorak, which made his already plump body look rotund. He had gloves. His thick, short, dark hair was like a fur hat, and didn't need a cover. He went downstairs, and arranged with Keith to be away for an hour, and Kay, the receptionist, let him out of the front door.

David was one of half a dozen residents whose convalescence was nearly complete. He was allowed to decide his own activities, and go out for a walk alone. He had to keep a promise to return at a time agreed with the shift manager. He walked slowly, and hesitantly, because he had one leg slightly shorter than the other, as a result of fractured bones. He also had a number of metal plates and pins in his thighs and hips, which were sometimes painful.

Once outside, the chilly sea breeze hit him, and he began to scout the grounds of Denby Hall. 'Denby Hall' was a grandiose name, attractive on notepaper. In reality, the Hall was a wind-blasted, fifty year old, shed-like wooden structure, with rooms for forty residents and staff on three floors. The building, with its faded terracotta paint, was lodged on a tussocky piece of south coast land, which sloped towards the water, then fell for a hundred feet in a sheer chalk cliff. It was at the edge of the town. The grounds had some sheltered areas of weedy grass, with ill-kept flower borders. The brick walls and terraces were crumbling. The garden was too exposed to grow anything less hardy than gorse, flax, and a few stunted pines. David's search of this scanty landscape did not take long.

He found Poppy behind the garages, near the rubbish bins, tied to a wooden pallet. She was a powerful dog, and had managed to drag the pallet a few yards. He talked to her from a distance to be assured of her good nature. David had no experience of dogs at all, that he could recall, and some slight fear of them. Seeing nothing but warmth in the amber eyes, he stepped forward, and released her. He took the leash, which Keith had improvised – an old leather waist-belt threaded through her collar – and led her away.

Along the cliff, the path parted from the busy road, and was quieter. On one side the sea hushed; on the other there was a grassy bank. David and the dog walked together for twenty minutes. Then pellets of rain started driving in from the south. Poppy was joyful, tugging at the leash, and wagging her tail energetically. David's legs, in jeans, were wet and chilled after a while. He kept his head down, and his eyes on the daisies in the grass, which were being lashed by the wind. He tried to concentrate on what he should do with Poppy. This really came down to tying her up again to await Keith's action, or letting her go.

David couldn't work out why Poppy had run away from Cathy's husband. He had known Desmond almost as long as he had known Cathy. Desmond thought that 'Dog' as he always called Poppy, wasn't worth all the bother it took to look after her. It didn't make a lot of sense to David to return Poppy to Desmond, if she didn't want to be with him, and he didn't want her. Presumably this was what Keith would do.

When they were near to Denby Hall, on a sudden impulse, David freed Poppy, and tossed the leash behind a bush. He did this without thinking that he was interfering in other people's lives, or doing something, apparently trifling, which might have bad consequences. In an imprecise way, he thought he was doing something positive for Cathy.

2

Before Poppy appeared at Denby Hall, Desmond had told David that he would soon make a visit with his solicitor to 'square up Cathy's affairs'. Desmond wanted David to be present to witness her will, and other documents.

"I'll get Rose or Keith as well," he said.

Desmond's visits to Cathy, apart from being sparse, had settled into a routine. He avoided mealtimes, and thus the performance of sitting in the dining room, listening to Mark Demeter, and others. He showed some distaste at either feeding Cathy with a spoon himself, or watching her being fed by a carer. He usually came in the mid-afternoon, at afternoon tea time, and had a cup of tea with her in the sitting room. He was at least prepared to manage Cathy's non-spill mug for her. Often, David joined them. Desmond liked having David there. He was somebody to talk to, who knew the practices at Denby Hall, and could help with the wheelchair.

After afternoon tea, Cathy would be taken away by a care assistant for a cigarette, and when she was returned David might play a tune on the piano, or the three of them would go to Cathy's room and listen to a Freddie Mercury CD. Cathy always chose Freddie, and it was the high point of her day, judging by her smiles, and excitement.

Desmond was bored with playing the CDs and DVDs in Cathy's room. He had long since given up buying new ones, because Cathy only wanted the old songs. He said to

David that he had heard Queen's greatest hits so often, that the sound tracks were scored into his brain. Cathy never got tired of Queen, and had their work played to her over and over again, through all her years at Denby Hall. Desmond tolerated these sessions, only rising occasionally from his chair. He would prowl around the room, looking in drawers, and the wardrobe, pulling out items of clothing, and examining them, studying the labels on the toilet articles in the shower cubicle, and reading old postcards he had seen more than once before.

On the day of Poppy's appearance, Desmond arrived with a Mr Piper. The solicitor was dark suited, with a saturnine complexion, and a fat neck, choked in a shirt, with a club tie. David met them at the door. As they went through the lobby on their way to Cathy's room, Mr Piper appeared to tip-toe, looking cautiously about himself at every step, turning his whole body rather than his head. Barney Colas, a long term inmate, accosted him, a hand on his arm.

"I know you," Barney said, "you're from Belize, aren't you? Just over on business?"

Barney, dressed in an orange singlet, and khaki shorts, did not look as serious as he sounded.

Mr Piper, who was from Drummond's Chambers, Beach Street, Brighton, veered away from Barney, and hurried up the stairs behind Desmond, without answering.

In a quiet way, Desmond managed the people he wanted present in Cathy's room; David and Keith, one of the shift managers. Keith's usual restless desire to be doing something, was stilled. The set of Desmond's face, with his penetrating, almost black eyes, hawk nose and sallow skin, was one of sincerity. On Cathy's dresser, the silver framed studio photograph of Desmond, with sleek black hair, which curled at the nape of his neck, looked out earnestly.

David decided he would say nothing about Poppy's appearance, and clearly he could not disclose his own hand in the affair. He thought no further ahead than enabling Cathy and Poppy to meet in the next few days.

Mr Piper addressed them, unfolding a heavy, bluish piece of paper on a table, cleared and placed beside Cathy's wheelchair.

"Mrs Marsden, I have drawn up your will in accordance with what I understand …"

"I gave you her instructions," Desmond said.

"Mrs Marsden …?" Mr Piper said to Cathy.

Cathy was looking out of the window. The pigeons across the road were fluttering, and then sweeping across the skyline in ragged formations.

"Carry on, William," Desmond said.

Mr Piper scowled, and looked at the document. "In this will you are leaving everything to your husband, and it differs from your previous will only in omitting your brother and sister as small beneficiaries."

"Hardly been to see her. Amazing, isn't it? Miserable …" Desmond said to David and Keith.

Mr Piper placed the document on, rather than in, Cathy's hands, which were not receptive.

"Please read it."

Cathy did not look at him. She did not even appear to be listening.

"Don't bother with reading. It's all right. She already knows," Desmond said.

Mr Piper opened the will, and showed Cathy where to sign, but she looked the other way, and the will lay awkwardly, half folded beside her arm.

"She can't hold a pen," David said.

"That's no problem," Desmond said, genially. "Let me help you, my dear."

Desmond reached over Cathy, trapping her small hand, and the pen, in his large one, and moved it quickly across the paper in a semblance of a signature. "There!"

"Excellent. Now, will the witnesses please sign, adding their occupation and address?" Mr Piper asked.

Keith went first. David was troubled by having to record his occupation. He looked uncertainly at Mr Piper.

"Just put clerk," Mr Piper suggested.

"But he's not a clerk," Keith said.

"What is he, then?" Mr Piper asked, his neck quivering at this intervention.

"He's unemployed," Keith said.

"That's not a very... that gives an unfortunate impression."

"Nothing to be ashamed of in being unemployed, if you are," Keith said.

"I'm a patient in a neurological disability home," David said.

"That's not an occupation," Mr Piper said.

"It is for some people," Keith said.

"'Unwaged' is better, or 'job-seeker'," Mr Piper said, with finality.

"Balls," Keith said.

"Put 'unemployed', David," Desmond intervened, soothingly.

Mr Piper expelled a loud sigh, and explained that the next document was a short deed in which Cathy gave to Desmond, *here and now,* all the money and other property she expected to get from her aunt, when her aunt died.

"Of course there are gift duty implications..." Mr Piper began.

"Let's skip that," Desmond said.

David already knew about this from Cathy. The aunt was a fragile old lady of ninety-five living in a residential home in

Hove. When Cathy had been a student at Edinburgh University, a wealthy woman professor of sociology had taken a liking to her. Impressed by Cathy's sporting prowess, as well as her studies, the professor had boasted that she would keep Cathy in tennis balls for the rest of her life. In fact, she died quite soon after this promise, leaving Cathy a small sum in cash. But the rest of the professor's property, an estate in the Peak district, was left to Cathy's aunt for her life. Only after the aunt's death, would it come to Cathy. The aunt, at ninety-five was now nearing the end of her span. The estate would soon come to Cathy. Cathy had told David that it was worth a lot of money, but she had no idea how much. She had only mentioned the bequest vaguely to Desmond when they married, because it had seemed so far in the future. Desmond had, however, become very concerned about it when Cathy moved to Denby Hall.

When Mr Piper asked Cathy to sign the second document which he had unfolded, she was equally unable to hold the pen. Desmond bent forward again, offering to help. He took Cathy's hand, but she angrily swiped it aside. The pen, and the deed, were knocked on to the floor.

"My dear…"

"Arrrrgh!"

"My dear, this is something we discussed and planned. You know there's no point in the money coming to you. If it does, it'll end up in the pocket of the Chancellor of the Exchequer. Come what may, you're going to be well looked after for the rest of your days."

Cathy looked at him sourly.

"David, you have a try," Desmond asked, picking up the pen and paper.

David tried to get Cathy's hand, and the pen, over the document. Cathy did not resist, but the result was a few unrecognisable squiggles on the paper. Desmond tried once more, only to be angrily rejected. David made a second attempt, and produced more squiggles. Cathy sat in imperious silence throughout this performance.

Mr Piper picked up the deed and looked at it closely.

"I believe we have enough here to regard it as Mrs Marsden's signature, albeit somewhat sketchily done!" he beamed.

Desmond turned to Keith and David, and spoke in emollient tones.

"I hope you'll understand the difficulties we have in arranging Cathy's affairs. Of course, all this has been fully discussed with her over quite a period."

He asked Keith and David to sign again as witnesses.

Keith looked around with wide eyes, his mouth hanging open slackly, as he bent over the document, and said, "You're sure this is all right?"

Desmond smiled feebly.

"Perfectly, my boy," Mr Piper said.

3

In the afternoon, David went to the kitchens. He persuaded Sally, the cook, to supply scraps of meat, and a plastic bowl for water. He told her candidly that he wanted to feed a dog, and she didn't mind. She had already had a glimpse of Poppy, and heard the story. Poppy's arrival was like seeing a flight of geese, or a school of dolphins, or a wedding party. Everybody had brightened, and talked with each other about it.

"I'm not sure that beauty eats ordinary meat, unless it's fillet steak cooked rare," Sally said, "but I'll give you something."

She heaved a leg of beef out of the chiller, and cut off two thick red slabs. David wrapped them in a newspaper. He obtained another hour's leave from Keith, and went outside. After he had wandered around the grounds, and along the nearby road, Poppy suddenly broke cover and bounded alongside him. He coaxed her back to a sheltered place behind the Hall's garages. He fed her and put out the bowl, filled with water from the garden tap. Poppy ate hungrily, and drank all the water.

"I don't know what I'm going to do about you, but stick around, and when the weather warms, maybe tomorrow, I'll bring Cathy outside, and we can have a walk together," he said to her.

David's idea, that he would be able to spend time with Poppy and Cathy in the grounds, was not very well thought through. Poppy could not be expected to disappear and reappear conveniently, and temporarily. She now raced around him, bouncing and barking, celebrating her liberty. She fell in at his heels, and followed him. This was dangerous. He stopped out of sight of the windows of the Hall.

"You can't go any further with me, or they'll catch you, and tie you up again."

The dog mewled in response, but continued alongside. With his deadline expiring, David patted her head. "I've got to go, but I'll be back."

The door was opened by Maggie, David's key worker – the person who kept an eye on his particular case – thin as a match under her blue workshirt.

"Hey, David. Greyfriars Bawbee is still around!"

Maggie had a wicked look that said, 'Shall we let her inside?' And she might have done so, until Mark Demeter appeared from the hall.

"Achtung! Herr Oberlieutenant approaches," he said, and Maggie shut the door.

Helmut, the proprietor of Denby Hall, came into the lobby. Helmut halted and watched. The dog squatted on the porch, head on one side, questioningly. David decided to get Cathy. He rescued her from the smoking room, and pushed her into the lobby. Poppy was still sitting. She yelped, and pawed the tiles at the sight of Cathy. Cathy's face rippled with suppressed or inexpressible emotion, but other than a throaty sound, she was quiet.

Helmut saw Cathy's reaction. He patted Cathy's shoulder.

"Vee can't let her inside," he said, regretfully.

He had obviously heard about Poppy's earlier visit, and David thought that Helmut, who was regarded as a kind of guru, as well as the boss, was an essential part of any plan to enable Cathy to see Poppy regularly.

Helmut Schniewind was universally known, and

addressed as Helmut, by residents, staff, health officials, and everybody else who came into contact with Denby Hall. Most residents had no idea of his last name. Some of the more savvy ones sometimes imitated his German accent, as Mark Demeter had attempted. David did not know whether the use of his first name was an act of friendliness, or because 'Mr Schniewind' sounded rather ugly. Perhaps it was both. David thought Helmut would have liked to be Dr Schniewind, but he wasn't a doctor of medicine, even though he looked and acted like one. He had a card on a chain around his neck, and a complicated looking mobile phone in his pocket. He was, however, closely involved in the therapeutic work. It was because Helmut was often hovering over the residents' treatments, that David drew this conclusion about an unfulfilled wish to be a doctor. Helmut didn't know all the residents personally, as Rose, and Keith and Ian the other shift manager, did – Helmut had another neuro-disability home in Kent to look after – but he was often amongst them, talking with residents, and listening to staff.

Helmut was in his late forties. His complexion was stained and lined like a tobacco leaf. His eyes often resolved to narrow slits, which gave him a good-humoured look. His manner was quiet. He had thin, slicked back grey hair and he dressed in off-whites, fawns and beiges. His jackets – he always wore a jacket and tie – fitted his slim figure well; he had a silk handkerchief in his breast pocket, and he wore soft moccasins. Helmut looked dashing most of the time, but occasionally, if he was overcome by a problem, his elegant clothes seemed drab and faded.

What was remarkable to David, and his friends amongst the more able-minded inmates, was that Helmut had enthused the staff, in a way which enabled them, at most times, to pass through the barrier that surrounded the disabled, and cut them off from people 'out there'. Training was too mundane a word to describe the gift Helmut had bestowed on the staff. He had imbued them with the ability to move across the chasm between the universe of those who are fit and well, and the many universes of the disabled. David could see the staff making this flight many times each day and night, back and forth. He knew how difficult the journey was, from his talks with Caroline and his father. Inevitably, there were times when the staff were confused about which universe they were in. The logic and sense which guided Denby Hall was not always that which applied outside its doors.

David, when he was standing in the grounds, and reading the noticeboard which advertised a 'Home for mostly mobile patients with neurological disabilities,' could see that from the outside, Denby Hall appeared to be a place of sadness and misfortune. Inside, under Helmut's influence, the atmosphere was light-hearted, one of amused tolerance. Beside the usual schedule of therapeutic classes, there were lots of meetings, talks, concerts, parties, singing and even dancing, which included those who were wheelchair-bound.

The décor of the Hall was faded, the wallpaper scuffed, the carpets worn and stained, and the rickety furniture seemed to have been assembled from a flat-pack by somebody who had lost a few critical screws. But there were vases of fresh flowers, pots of green plants, and bright pictures painted by the residents on the walls. Denby Hall was suffused by a culture of acceptance of what happened in the moment, which warmed David, and all the other residents. Helmut was acknowledged as the author of this. The ethos of Denby Hall emanated from him.

While they were staring at the dog, Keith came dashing through the lobby muttering to himself, and saw Poppy outside.

"Dammit, the beast is back!"

He diverted his course, headed for the door, and keyed in the combination of numbers for the lock. He let himself out, disregarding the rain, which quickly soaked his blue check uniform shirt once he was beyond the porch. Poppy was wary of him now and ran off a few yards, before turning to watch him. Poppy retreated as Keith advanced, until they were both out of sight of the windows.

Helmut turned away, to go back to his room. "Iss a beautiful animal," he said to Cathy and David, "but vee have to send it away."

David had decided as he watched, that he had to do something more about Poppy. It was not satisfactory that the dog should be returned to Desmond, and the book closed. He was irritated at his own inability to work out what to do. He pushed Cathy's wheelchair into the games room. It was empty because the residents were mostly in classes, painting, modelling, listening to music, or receiving different treatments, and therapies. Cathy could not now follow this schedule of events even passively. Her disease made her disruptive at times. Her suspension from the daily schedule also signalled the possibility that she could be sent away from Denby Hall. It was a deep worry of hers which she had communicated to David. He was a different case, free to attend, or develop his own pursuits.

"Do you want me to try to keep Poppy here so that you can see her?" David asked her.

Cathy assented strongly to this, her chest heaving. "Mmmmmmmmh!"

David thought that he was probably undertaking a task he could not complete, and really had no clear idea how to perform. He simply felt impelled to do it if he could.

David had never thought about the implications of keeping pets in a care home for people with neurological problems. Rose was probably right about having a dog indoors, but he thought it might be possible to keep Poppy in the grounds of Denby Hall. All that was necessary was a kennel, and arrangements for regular dog-food and water. Or, if Poppy was lodged at the local kennels, it might be possible for him to bring her to see Cathy. But lodging at the kennels would cost money, and other than a small sum of pocket money, he had nothing.

Later in the day, David managed to get Keith's attention. Keith was usually tensely preoccupied with several tasks at once. He would give orders, all at the same time, to different members of staff, break off to counsel a resident, or talk on a mobile phone. He rushed from one fuss in the Hall to another. But he was always jovial, bantering as he moved, and he could be halted. Keith knew every resident by first name, and remembered a lot of personal things about each one of them. David stopped dead in front of Keith in the corridor, blocking his path.

"What's the trouble, David?" he asked, his eyes and mouth wide open in his long, vertically lined face.

Keith had a way of concentrating on a resident expectantly. It was slightly unnerving, but meant kindly. A resident could certainly get a hearing, but Keith was a hard man to fool.

"The d-dog ..."

"Couldn't catch it again. Too cunning. The dog's gone, David. Vanished. Vamoosed. Why do you want to know?"

David decided not to mention his part in Poppy's freedom. "It's Cathy's."

Keith considered this seriously, and then he said, "Naaah. As far as I know, the dog lives at some number I've forgotten in Eccleston Street. People by the name of Temple. And that's not where Cathy used to live. That's not her husband's address."

21

David was startled, and moved his head negatively.

"I'm right, David. The dog's collar. There's an owner's name and address tag on it."

David hadn't looked at Poppy's collar. In fact he hadn't considered that Poppy might be somebody else's property.

"If it's the same dog, the one Cathy used to have, it's been sold," Keith said

"C-can … we keep her in the grounds, if she's run away and come back to Cathy?" David persisted.

Keith's eyes flicked in different directions, and he scratched his oily hair. He was no expert on the terms of Denby Hall's licence.

"Naah, you couldn't keep her here anyway. Bound to be something in the small print about keeping animals."

"The r-residents would love her."

"Not practical, David. Maybe some would love her. But some might be scared."

"Is there anything we can do?"

Keith's head lolled, considering. "I don't see it. If the dog hasn't already decided for itself that a warm kennel in Eccleston Street is better than a cold hillside, we'll have to return her. Can't see any other way."

The way Keith said it, and David understood it, the new owner won, but only by a narrow margin. But the problem, for David, had become more complicated. Now, it wasn't merely a matter of persuading Desmond that it would be good for Cathy to see the dog. Now, there was a new owner to be dealt with. The chances of persuading the buyer to let Cathy see the dog occasionally were probably slim, but David was determined to try. That Desmond had sold Poppy, only inflamed his determination.

4

Although Keith had suggested that the dog might not have originally been Cathy's, David had no doubt. If Poppy's owner was now Temple, of a strange address, then Cathy's husband had sold the dog, and it had escaped from its new owner.

To David, it seemed unkind to have sold the dog, or at least to have sold it without telling Cathy. But Desmond, like David's father and Caroline Higgins, was a universe away. David was sure Desmond would justify his action as reasonable, although it did not seem that way to David. Dealing with the dog would be trivial to Desmond, because he had already made the ultimate decision about Cathy. She had explained it vividly to David not long after they met. She described a meeting with Desmond in the Denby Hall garden.

The garden was an overgrown and wild place, but on a clear, still day in summer, you could see through and beyond the twisted pines, with their thin needles, to a triangle of sea, and a limitless sky. Cathy was in her wheelchair, and Desmond was sitting on a stone wall beside a bedraggled border of geraniums. He looked out of place in a silk tie, and a dark business suit, which clung to his tall body. Desmond usually dressed as though he had called in on the way to another meeting. He was anxious to leave. He had what Cathy had described as his 'Things are not going fast enough' manner. His fingers clenched and unclenched with impatience. Desmond had said that Dr Floor, the doctor in charge at Denby Hall, 'wanted to be clear about something'.

'You see, Cathy, if you were to have a stroke, or a massive incident...'

'What's a massive incident?' she had asked.

'I'm not sure. Doctor-speak for a heart attack, I think. A big one. If you had one of those, you could be ... damaged.'

'But I'm already damaged.'

'I mean you might end up like a daffodil or a starfish.'

'That would be nice, actually.'

'You wouldn't have any quality of life.'

'What's wrong with a daffodil's quality of life?'

'Don't be silly, Cathy. You're a woman of experience.'

'A daffodil is alive.'

Irritated, Desmond had plugged on. 'You know that the medical profession are too clever. They can prolong life indefinitely, when life is no more than a heartbeat. You used to be very pragmatic about this before you became ill. There has to be a point where one says to doctors, *Do not resuscitate.*'

'That was before I became ill.'

'It's a question of what is rational, Cathy. That doesn't change because a person becomes ill.'

'But it does, Desmond.'

'I'm sorry, my dear, but you're talking... You're not making any sense.'

'How do you know whether a sick person is feeling anything?'

'When the brain is dead...'

'Suppose the brain is mostly, but not quite dead.'

Desmond snorted, 'You can quibble about all sorts of cases, but...'

'So if anything happens, I'm gone.'

'Basically... that's right.'

'And you've already given Dr Floor his instructions, *Do not resuscitate?*'

'He asked me, and I told him.'

'Did he ask what I wanted?'

'Yes, and I told him.'

'Desmond, whose life is it?'

'My dear, I'm talking it over with you now, aren't I?'

'Thank you for that. I think you're telling me.'

'Reminding, really.'

'Wrong, Desmond. Remind is the wrong word. You see, I do have a different mind now. You've seen the brain scan. I can't be re-minded. I wish I could.'

'Cathy, you're playing with words.'

'Have you talked to my brother?'

'On the phone. He agrees.'

'Do you think Simon counts?'

'How do you mean?' Desmond asked.

'My brother, whom I haven't seen for years, pronouncing on my life or death from a distance.'

'Simon is a creep, but he's your brother.'

'And Denise?'

'I sent your dear sister an email, and she never replied. Never does.'

'That would be Denise.' ·

'This is the right thing, Cathy.'

'You'll be able to take over the property if I have an *incident.*'

'Our property has nothing to do with it.'

'Imagine if I had an incident, and became unconscious, a starfish or a daffodil, for years and years.'

'I want to spare you that, Dear.'

'Then you might die before me, Desmond, and my money would go to pay my hospital bills, and Anita would get nothing.'

'Please. Anita doesn't come into this.'

"You see, David," Cathy said, when she had finished the story, "Desmond doesn't credit me with any preference, even over my own life."

Anita seemed to be a haunting presence in all of Cathy's talk about her past, but otherwise, Cathy didn't seem too agitated about this conversation. She even joked to David about the blue ticket she would have on her bed, and wheelchair. 'And why blue? Shouldn't it be black?' she asked.

"Do you want me to speak to Keith or Rose or Helmut about it?" David had asked.

He ruled out Dr Floor who, although sympathetic, did not seem to have the antenna to receive any information, other than in answer to his own questions.

"I'm not sure they'll listen to you. I'll think about it," Cathy said.

"I'll speak," David insisted, feeling the need to help, but knowing, at the same time, that they certainly wouldn't listen to him.

"I'll think about it first."

But Cathy never returned to the subject. If Desmond could tell Dr Floor *Do not resuscitate Cathy*, it didn't surprise David, that he could sell Poppy at any moment he liked, without feeling accountable to Cathy. Desmond prided himself on his propriety, and he would be offended if David said he was being unkind. He would take refuge in 'common sense.'

5

David noticed that as Cathy's illness advanced, she took less interest in her appearance. When she arrived at the Hall, she brought with her a red, silk-covered box full of costume jewellery, bracelets, and rings. She had some necklaces made by indigenous people in North and South America, Asia and Australia, collected on her travels with Desmond. She delighted, at first, in dressing up, and wearing her trinkets; but after about two years, she hardly seemed to care. David became aware that she scarcely ever looked at herself in the mirror. Desmond had ensured that Cathy had her profuse and wild hair coloured and cut from time to time, but eventually, even when it was showing an inch of grey at the roots, she did not appear to notice. However, Desmond was quite open about wanting his wife's hair dressed, because any neglect might be attributed to him.

He complained to David about the difficulty of taking Cathy to the hairdresser. On at least one previous occasion, when David had been present, Cathy had been refused service. The hairdresser, had said primly, after a few snips, that such a customer was too difficult for her.

"It's a trial," Desmond said to David, "The hairdressers don't like it. Everything gets very awkward, you know, with Cathy jerking around. I swore that the last time would be the last. There are a number of salons around the town that I wouldn't like to go back to. But one or two of the girls, here at the Hall, have been saying to me that it would be good for

Cathy to have her hair done. They see the grey streaks. They don't think about the difficulties of doing the job, of course! I don't know. Perhaps I'll give it one more go."

Cathy showed, if not excitement, then at least satisfaction at the prospect of a hairdo, 'the works' as she used to call it, which meant a colour, wash, cut and dry. With the help of Kay, Desmond found that there was a salon they had never offended before, at the edge of the housing estate, half a mile away. Desmond and David arrived for the appointment in the Hall's minibus, with Cathy in her chair. They unloaded her, and wheeled her into Darren's Hair & Beauty.

The salon was in a short row of shops which had been artificially placed, rather than attracted by commerce, not too many years before, to serve the adjoining council estates. Like the newsagent's, the wine shop, the Indian grocery and the fish and chip shop, Darren's Hair & Beauty had a façade of dusty glass, flaking paint, and graffiti-daubed red brick.

"Scruffy place," Desmond muttered as they entered. "Mostly clientele from the estate." The two chairs were already occupied by women. Both the hairdressers were men. One, with only a few threads of hair himself, wore a scarlet athletic singlet, which left his shoulders, and much of his chest bare. He was clipping absent-mindedly over his customer. At the same time, he was holding a conversation with a youth of about eighteen, who sat on the waiting bench, with a bulldog pup on his lap. The youth fondled the pup, and at times lifted it up to kiss its wrinkled face, and smooth his cheek along its furry flank.

The other hairdresser made an agreeable movement of his head when Cathy was wheeled in. "Take a pew. With you in a moment," he said.

He had 'Darren Moreno' stitched on the breast pocket of his smock. He was a small man with hunched shoulders, not much taller than his customer, as she sat in the chair. His crinkled black hair was oiled, and stuck out raggedly all over his head.

"Can't help noticing the hair," Desmond said, in a low voice to David. "An omen."

On one side of the salon, a girl with dreadlocks, and tanned legs bursting out of a short leather skirt, was placing fingernail extensions on a woman customer's hand. The woman's hand, resting on a curved stand, had five long, blue claws.

When Darren had finished the blow dry, and ceremoniously seen his customer off the premises, he returned to the main floor, bowed at Cathy, and gestured to his chair. David could see the dilemma developing in the hairdresser's mind. Should Cathy move to the barbering chair? Could she be moved? If not, could she remain in the wheelchair? Darren's hands caressed the air, as his glance shot from barber's chair to wheelchair, and back, several times.

"I think, my love, we'll leave you in the wheelchair, nice and comfortable like," Darren said with professional confidence, a decision which was eased by his own short stature.

Desmond placed the wheelchair before the mirror, and braked it. "I'm afraid Cathy moves a bit."

"Cathy won't be a problem, will you sweetheart?" Darren said, swaying around her, flapping the cover sheet like a bullfighter's cloak.

He began to mix a black potion with a hint of red, darting to Cathy to examine, and run his hand through her hair, as he changed the colour of the mix slightly to make a match. At last he declared it perfect, and advanced on her, his hands full with the brush for the colour, a comb, and clips. Cathy stared straight ahead, expressionless.

Darren combed a parting in Cathy's hair where the grey hair from the roots was exposed. He held it open with a clip, and quickly dabbed on the colour. It was an operation which required dexterity, even if the customer sat perfectly still. But Cathy did not sit still. The task facing Darren, was to repeat this process fifty, a hundred or more times. As he progressed gamely, the movements of Cathy's head splattered the dye over her forehead, and in her ears, as well as on her hair.

Darren ragged Cathy, who now chuckled and sniggered. He challenged her to foil his strokes, dancing in to comb a few locks, retreating, then diving back to pin the parting, and at last rocking his shoulders, and completing the dab of dye with his brush.

The man in the red singlet finished his customer, and went outside with the youth for a smoke, leaving the bulldog pup snuffling on the seat. The animal cocked its eye at Darren's ballet act, and particularly at the trailing cover sheet, as Darren, who had unbraked the chair, swung Cathy around.

The dog jumped down from the seat, grabbed the sheet in its jaws, and started to run around, turning the chair. Cathy leaned over giggling, enjoying the merry-go-round, and this seemed to encourage the animal. The dog pulled Cathy's cover sheet off. The dye jar in Darren's hand was upset over her clothes, as he tried to resist. The man in the red singlet and the youth rushed in to help. They tried to catch the dog, which hung on to the sheet with determination. The three of them, the red-singlet man, the youth, and Darren, ended on the floor in a mess of dye, with Cathy chortling in the chair, looking like an Afro-Caribbean.

The youth took the bulldog in his arms, and kissed it as though it was the injured party. Darren, with resignation, cleaned Cathy up as best he could. Nothing could remove the brown blob, as big as a saucer, from the front of her pea green t-shirt, or the dark stains from her forehead and cheeks.

"Sorry about that, mate," he said to Desmond, "but what can y'do?"

"Cathy's having fun," David said.

Desmond ground his teeth, and whispered to David, "What he could do, is keep bloody bulldogs out of his beauty salon!"

When the colour had set, Cathy was manhandled by Darren and Desmond to the hairwash basins in the next room. Getting Cathy to bend over backwards wasn't easy, but Darren was persuasive, and after the wash she was returned to the cutting chair.

As Darren began to comb and snip, Cathy began to roll her head. He tried holding her head still with one hand, but she shook herself free. The more Cathy moved, the more determined Darren seemed to be. He darted forward and back, like a swordsman, even at times cheering himself on, as he made a difficult snip. He stepped back at times to survey his work, wriggling his hips, with his legs apart, to determine where he was going to strike next. "Oh – ah! – yes – now! – got you!" he laughed, as he dodged around the wheelchair.

While this performance was going on, the hairdresser in the scarlet singlet disappeared with the youth and the bulldog. Another customer arrived, a thirtyish woman in a tight, pink dress, dotted with silver stars, more suitable for a nightclub than a hot afternoon in a dilapidated suburban street. She stood in front of the mirrors, pleased with her figure, and watched Cathy's cut. She lit a cigarette, ignoring the no-smoking sign. She glanced pointedly at her wristwatch, and began tapping the toe of her high-heeled foot on the tiled floor.

"What about my appointment, then?" she said, after a minute.

"With you in a moment, dear lady," Darren smiled.

He snipped a little more, set down his comb and scissors on the bench, and calmly took the woman into the hair-wash room. He came back a moment later.

"I've told my assistant to drown her," he said, and returned to his task with concentration.

When Cathy's blow-dry was done, Desmond paid the bill with a large tip. Cathy did not seem to see her new self.

"You sir, have the patience of a saint," Desmond said to Darren.

"No way, mate," Darren said, "I had my mum in a wheelchair. Like that. Doolally for years."

David wheeled Cathy outside to wait for the minibus which Desmond had called on his mobile.

"That, I swear, was Cathy's final hairdo, absolutely, positively the last!" Desmond said.

David didn't know whether Cathy understood this declaration, but he said, "I'm sure you'd like to see Darren again, wouldn't you, Cathy?"

Desmond went on, regardless of Cathy, "We were lucky with that man, but the fussing hasn't made any difference to Cathy. OK, she looks a bit younger. And she appears to have changed her ethnic origin. But she doesn't know anything about it."

"But you enjoyed the bulldog bit, didn't you," David said, to Cathy.

Desmond wrinkled his nose at something rancid.

6

The morning was cloudy, with a sharpness in the air, but the wind had dropped. Keith judged it was suitable for David to take Cathy, well wrapped up, for an hour in the grounds. David's objective was to find Poppy if she had not been captured. He decided not to tell Cathy that Poppy had been sold, until he had exhausted every possibility of making an arrangement for Cathy to see her regularly.

David pushed the wheelchair along the gravel drive, and then over the lumpy lawn, past the row of pines, to the back of the garages, near the place where Poppy had first been tied. He told Cathy that this was where he had fed Poppy last night. He whistled a few times, and called Poppy's name. To their pleasure, Poppy found them. Leaping out of the hedge, she raised her muzzle over her teeth, in what Labrador owners call a smile, and jigged from one forepaw to another, before resting them on Cathy's lap. Cathy gurgled, and thrust about in her chair. When David patted Poppy he found she was cold and damp.

David thought that Keith had been wrong about Poppy being influenced by her own creature comforts. Eccleston Street might be warm and dry, but it didn't seem to matter to Poppy that Cathy couldn't speak, or feed her, or give her more than the occasional pat. Poppy was like the rough-sleeper's dog, happy alongside her master under a thin blanket, on a cold street in the rain. And David's own feeling for Cathy was something like that; a simple thread of attraction which defied explanation. It simply *was*. Cathy radiated a force, which was not domination or control – these were beyond her – even when she was silent in her wheelchair. People noticed her, were attracted to her, and often deferred to her.

David saw that Keith had come outside, and was talking to the driver of a truck which had stopped in front of the garages. He was giving the driver instructions about moving boxes of supplies into storage in one of the garages. He had seen David, Cathy – and Poppy, and when he had finished talking to the driver, he walked toward them, looking composed.

"Going to take the dog for a walk?" Keith said cheerfully, as though there had been no trouble with Poppy, and she was Cathy's pet.

"Yes," David said. "I found her …"

"You know she'll follow you to the Hall when you come back. Helmut will see her, and he'll say she has to go."

Fortunately, Keith didn't say anything about a new owner.

"Helmut won't see her, if I tie her up here," David said.

"You shouldn't do that, David. We'll only get into trouble."

David wasn't too bothered about 'getting into trouble' himself, whatever that meant. He was probably already in trouble for freeing and feeding Poppy. But he appreciated that Keith was suggesting that Denby Hall would suffer. He didn't want that. And he didn't want to displease Helmut.

David wheeled Cathy off for their walk, with Poppy padding alongside. The cliff path was deserted, and the sea had calmed into rippled oil, which made their eyes water. The wild flowers were standing up in the tussock; buttercups and ragged robin as well as daisies. Cathy made occasional gestures toward Poppy, flopping her arm on to Poppy's shoulders. When David decided they had to turn back, he stopped, and gave Cathy a cigarette, holding it for her to puff.

He got supplies of cigarettes, and a lighter, from Kay whenever he took Cathy out. Poppy sat on her hind quarters watching patiently.

David made no attempt to get rid of Poppy, or tie her up as they approached the Hall on their return. As Keith had said, Helmut would see them, and he soon came out on to the porch. He looked regretful. Keith was behind him.

"Please," Helmut said. "Vee cannot keep the dog here. I'm sorry."

"It's tough, Cathy, I know," Keith said, making an unsuccessful grab at Polly who quickly backed away.

Cathy couldn't say anything. She watched round-eyed as Keith failed to trap the dog in another move. David reluctantly accepted the situation, and pushed the wheelchair up the ramp on to the porch.

Helmut raised his palms in a hopeless gesture, looking less jaunty than usual, with his flat-footed loafers, and chair-creased trousers. "Vee'll get in trouble!"

Once, David overheard his father in the next room, telling family friends with characteristic candour: 'David's a testament to the brilliance of modern surgery. The medics scraped him up from the asphalt, and the surgeons screwed him together. Sadly, I sometimes think …'

David never heard the end of that sentence. He liked to think that his father drew back from uttering the words, 'It would have been kinder to let David die.' He knew his father was a man with a generous heart, and hoped he was really only saying, or perhaps implying, that from his own point of view – the view of a person with his mental and physical faculties intact – his father would rather be dead.

His father, a property surveyor in private practice, would, David thought, have been tolerant with a son who was a low achiever. But David's musical skills, before the accident, had convinced his father that he had a brilliant son. And it was difficult for David, and his father, to appreciate how far the trauma had moved David beyond the likelihood of any kind of achievement in his father's sphere – the university educated world of business, and professional careers. It was a bitter uncertainty for David. Equally, to his father, David seemed to inhabit a space that he could hardly penetrate. Hence his father's frown of confusion and the fishy, unfocussed look in his eye, when he visited Denby Hall. They were reaching out to each other, and falling short.

In the years of recuperation at Denby Hall, David had gained a measure of detached acceptance of his plight. Cathy had helped him. She had once called them, 'A man without a past, and a woman without a future, together on an island of misunderstanding.'

David thought his present existence was quite pleasant and interesting. He never speculated whether it would be better to be dead. His 'being' confirmed that it was good to be alive. Yes, there was pain from his back and legs, but he had pills for that. The fact that he couldn't always work out very quickly, or accurately, what was happening around him wasn't such a handicap now that he had become used to it.

Caroline had tried to get him to resume studies, or at least the reading of books, and to take a part in social groups. He wanted to respond, but he could not find the will or the interest. His father accused David of having lost his sense of curiosity about distant people, and places. If he had had that curiosity in the past, it was true that it had now fallen below the horizon of his mind. Caroline hung her head when she failed to ignite a flash of interest about seeing Mt. Fuji, or the Galapagos. David knew they were wonderful places – he saw them on television – but he could not face what he feared would be the disorientation of foreign travel. He preferred quiet, immediate pursuits, like listening to music, or just sitting in a coffee shop, and watching the passers by.

What his father and Caroline couldn't understand, was that it was not painful or unpleasant to be deprived of the urge to travel, or the ability to read and study, or play the part in society that they thought he should play. He wasn't standing on a patch he regarded as deprived, and looking over the fence, aching for the things he didn't have. It was the other way round. He felt lucky to be alive. He now understood that even the most broken person at Denby Hall had a valuable spark of life. Even Cathy, who had the smallest spark imaginable. Playing tunes on the piano from the Hall's songbook, talking or communicating with somebody like Cathy, cooking the occasional meal in the residents' kitchen, joking with Mark Demeter and John Murdoch, and walking in the town, made a full life, and these things were just about the limit of what he could do. He had found that there was no hurt or anxiety in not doing what he couldn't do.

His father's objective before the accident – and his own – was that David would become a concert pianist, or at least that he would become a member of one of the prestigious nationally known symphony orchestras. Now it was like a distant star. And, sadly, as unattainable.

Eventually Poppy disappeared. David searched the grounds, and walked for half a mile each way along the cliff path several times. He whistled until his lips were chapped. He reasoned that Helmut's will had prevailed, and that Poppy had been delivered to her new owner. David made no explanation to Cathy. He had noted the exact address on Poppy's collar – 73 Eccleston Street – and he had an idea, although it was hard to screw up his determination to carry it out.

One morning he walked to Eccleston Street. It was wide and quiet, and lined with beech trees, a century old white-painted terrace of large houses, with columned porticos several steps up from street level. The ground and first floor windows – there were four floors – had tall panes of glass, which suggested reception rooms with elegantly plastered ceilings. Some houses had manicured plants, and flowers, in pots on their porches. This was an enclave of middle class homes, immaculately maintained.

David felt apprehensive, but he mounted the steps at number 73 resolutely, and pressed the bell. Poppy barked, and he heard the muffled thump of her paws on the carpet. A Filipino maid opened the door a crack, and Poppy poked her nose out, but a taller woman was at the maid's shoulder.

"Take Justina away, Maria," the woman said, occupying the space in the open doorway. "Now?" she added, as Poppy was led away, barking.

"I'm … David … from Denby Hall."

"Denby Hall? I was expecting the plumber."

"I've come about … Poppy."

Poppy was still barking in the depths of the house.

"Poppy? Poppy? There's nobody of that name here. You've got the wrong house."

She was a tall, slender woman, around forty, with a bony hand on one hip, and shoulder-length, lank, fair hair. She had a phlegmy voice, blue stains under her eyes, and a kind of beaten-up prettiness.

"The … the dog."

"Justina? Her name is Justina."

"I would like … to take her for a walk."

The woman had a wide, thin-lipped mouth which twitched at this information.

"How much do you charge?" she asked slyly.

David shook his head. "Nothing."

The woman's heavy eyelids drooped knowingly. "No thanks. I already have a dog-walker when I need one."

She backed into the hall, a hand on the door to close it. Poppy was still barking. David knew then that he had started in the wrong way, and given a wrong impression. He had sounded like a beggar or a thief.

"I would like to take her to see Cathy at Denby Hall," he blurted.

"Oh, you would, would you? Why didn't you say that in the first place?"

"I would walk Poppy ... Justina."

"But you really want to take her to Denby Hall. You want to take her away. That's where Justina was found."

"We didn't take her away ... sh-she ran away ... she came to the Hall."

"Now listen to me, Mr ... Justina is a very valuable thoroughbred dog, and she's not going near Denby Hall!"

The woman shut the door, and David had begun to ease himself down the steps, when he realised he had only explained a part of his idea. He heaved himself up to the door again, and pressed the bell. This time, the woman alone opened the door.

Her face lined more deeply when she saw it was David.

"Didn't I make myself clear?"

"S-Sorry ... Could I say, Justina used to be Cathy's dog."

"She's our family dog, and don't you interfere with her in any way!"

"But j-just for Cathy to see her occasionally," he pressed.

"She's our dog! Do you understand?"

"It would help Cathy."

"No. Don't take me for a fool. You'd never bring her back. And even if you did, Justina can't have two masters."

"Y-Yes," David said weakly. "She could. She wouldn't run away then."

"No! We're not into dog-sharing. Justina is ours!" the woman shouted, retreating impatiently, and slamming the door in his face.

David walked slowly back to Denby Hall, considering how perfect his solution had seemed to be, and yet apparently unworkable in practice, and, judging by Mrs Temple's attitude, almost offensive.

7

David told Cathy that he was still trying to make arrangements for her to see Poppy. He said nothing about Mrs Temple, or the Eccleston Street visit; it wasn't worth complicating Cathy's life. David was still feeling embarrassed at his misjudgment. Despite Mrs Temple's rejection of his proposal, he cast about for a different way to solve the problem. Perhaps if he met the dog-walker from Eccleston Street, and invited him to take a short detour via Denby Hall? It might work. His inconclusive thoughts ended in a headache.

That David's friendship with Cathy was unlikely, was hardly noticeable in a place where everything was unlikely. At first, there had been the fun of playing the piano together and singing; and then they had talked a lot, first about the Hall, and the characters around them, enjoying the moment together. Later, as Cathy's ability to speak began to deteriorate, she reminisced more and more about her past. She seemed to want to create a picture which satisfied her as accurate, pleasant or unpleasant, before her voice failed entirely; a kind of autobiography, which she was leaving with David. He watched her fatal disease progress relentlessly, month by month; the fading voice, the difficulty swallowing, the impossibility of controlling her limbs. But her mind in there, like a clam inside its shell, and with his methods, David could reach it.

David received Cathy's confidences uncritically, because

he had no past experience to test them against. He was, in Caroline's words, 'a blank sheet of paper'. If Caroline had known that somebody else was scribbling on what she regarded as 'her' blank sheet, she might have insisted to his father that David be moved. Caroline frequently enquired about his relationships at Denby Hall, and particularly his relationship with Cathy, because she knew that they were close. David merely sheltered behind his inarticulateness, and gave little away.

In the early days, David would sometimes go out with Cathy, Desmond, and a care assistant to lunch. Their favourite place was a few miles away from the Hall, the White Swan, a pub on the cliffs, high above the sea. On a fine day, it was an ideal place for Cathy, with easily accessible outdoor benches, and a vast view of the Channel, dotted with yachts and fishing boats. Whenever David asked Cathy whether she was enjoying the scene she usually said it was 'nice'. But even when the sun was shining, the wind could be unfriendly, tearing away paper napkins, and menu cards. Lighting one of Cathy's cigarettes could become a lengthy, and trying operation. Inside, the Swan was spacious and comfortable, with many alcoves for privacy.

Cathy's party usually opted for the inside of the White Swan, and this preference had been particularly prompted by an unfortunate event in the garden. The picnic area sloped slightly, and on one occasion Cathy's wheelchair, which was jammed against a bench, had freed itself while Desmond was away at the bar placing the order for lunch.

The wheelchair, of its own volition, had performed an unobtrusive backward circle, drawing Cathy quietly away from the table. David was talking to Beverly, the carer on duty, when they noticed the wheelchair. Cathy was facing the sea, with about twenty-five yards of bristly brown grass between her and the cliff edge. The chair started to run forward. Cathy had no sense of alarm, and even seemed to enjoy the prospect of rolling down the slope. She shouted encouragingly, and raised her clenched fist.

David could not extricate his legs from the bench very quickly without provoking pain, but he tried. Beverly, fortunately an athletic girl, sprang after Cathy. The wheelchair gained momentum, and the only way Beverly could stop it, was to sit down on the grass, and let the chair drag her body on the ground until it halted. She scrambled to her feet, and turned the wheelchair, with Cathy in good spirits.

Beverly had an audience. The guests at the other benches had looked up from their burgers and chips. As Beverly brushed herself down, they acknowledged her presence of mind with whistles, and noises of relief.

Desmond, coming down the slope with a tray of drinks, said, "Whatever happened to the bloody brakes?"

"They don't work," David said.

Desmond said something under his breath about the Hall costing a fortune, but not being able to provide a serviceable wheelchair. And that was more or less the end of al fresco lunches at the Swan.

The White Swan saw the end of lunches altogether, as a form of entertaining Cathy, several months later. Their party, including Desmond, Maggie and David had gathered at an inside table in a bay reserved for smokers. Cathy's chair, which she could still leave at this stage if there was somebody to support her, had been left outside. She was placed in a seat at the table. She had been given a cigarette, and was feeling in good humour. Still able to speak a few words, she began to chant words which David could identify as 'Scampi! Scampi!'

Patrons stared. The waitress, a local girl who was used to serving Denby Hall residents, grinned, and took their orders.

Desmond repeated his usual grouch about not being able to find anything on the menu which wasn't fried, or drenched in oil. But their orders were decided, and given. An awkward silence fell on their disparate party. Desmond was the dominating figure, and to engage Maggie, he observed how cold Glasgow was. "But it has a Gothic skyline," he said, as a saver. Maggie joked in reply, in her thick accent, and began to ask Cathy trivial questions, giving the replies herself, in the way that many people speak to those who are mute. The food was brought to them at last. Cathy, previously silent, hummed with pleasure when her plate of scampi and chips was placed in front of her. Maggie pushed her own sandwich aside, and began to cut Cathy's food into small fragments.

"Would you like tartare sauce?" Desmond asked Cathy.

The waitress brought the bowl of sauce, but before she could place it on the table, or Desmond could take it, Cathy threw out her arm involuntarily, knocking the bowl against the waitress's chest. The dish dropped to the floor, and broke. A glob of the white glutinous mixture, as big as a lemon, was deposited on the tanned cleft between the girl's breasts. The sauce began to run down the inside, and the outside, of her low cut black dress. And the backhand blow from Cathy obviously surprised, and hurt her. She squealed.

Maggie bobbed up with a handful of paper napkins, and began wiping the waitress's chest and dress. Desmond repeated 'sorry' countless times. Once more their party was the centre of covert attention. When the waitress had been quieted as much as possible, and had retired, Cathy ate a hearty portion from Maggie's spoon. The others, including David, picked at their orders. David never had an appetite on these occasions, although he was fond of scampi and chips. Desmond's unease always communicated to him like an electric current.

It was resolved between Maggie and Desmond, that Cathy would follow with sticky toffee pudding, but before this request could be placed, the manager visited their table. He was young and affable, with a shaven and shining head, and shoulders which bulged under his suit. Desmond shook hands with him as though he was a foreign potentate, and launched into an ode of regret, subtly flavoured with self-pity, for the plight of one who has to manage a disabled person. He also produced a twenty pound note for 'dry cleaning' which disappeared into the wide palm of the manager.

The manager was unperturbed. "We have a lot of people here from the Hall. We understand. We value the custom. Debbie isn't hurt, that's the main thing."

In this moment of peace, having achieved a perfect recovery, and with the manager about to depart following Desmond's second hand-shake, Cathy let out a loud, and very long fart.

"Oh, my God!" Desmond groaned, running his fingers through his hair in exasperation.

The manager affected not to hear, and backed away. An unsavoury smell engulfed the table.

"Are you all right, dear?" Maggie asked.

"Pooh," Cathy said.

"She needs to go to the toilet," David said.

"Oh, no! I thought … surely she wears a nappy?" Desmond said.

"She does," Maggie said, "but she needs changing, like a baby."

"But this never happened before, I mean …"

"Cheer up, Mr Marsden, shit happens!" Maggie said, holding up a plastic bag, with a spare nappy inside.

"What will we do?" Desmond asked, plaintively.

"I'll take her to the ladies' toilet, and try to clean her up, otherwise …you know it could be unpleasant and messy in your car," Maggie said.

"Can you manage her on your own?" David asked,

thinking that the slender Maggie seemed to have no strength for such a task.

"There's nobody else, is there?" she said, in a chirpy tone.

David began to foresee problems, but he didn't voice them because there was no solution. On this floor there was only one ladies' lavatory, which Cathy would have to occupy. The other lavatory, was a floor above, and there was no lift. It meant that the room on this level was in constant use. If Maggie went in there with Cathy, and Cathy wasn't cooperative, there would be a delay. Cathy sometimes resisted being handled by carers, and the acrobatics of changing her pants in a confined space were almost unimaginable.

Cathy was able to support herself, aided, for a few yards, and Maggie, with Desmond's help, got her to the door of the lavatory, which was within sight of their table. Desmond pushed Cathy and Maggie inside the door, closed it, and went to the bar where he ordered, and drank, a double whisky before returning to David.

David sat with Desmond while at least three women went into the lavatory, and came out immediately, looking uncomfortable and frowning.

"Something's gone wrong!" Desmond said, his mouth turned down.

After five minutes, Maggie came out of the lavatory on her own, looking worried. She came across to them.

"It's a hell of a mess in there. I can't get her clothes on. She's on the floor. She can't get up, and I can't lift her, and there's shit over everything, the floor, the walls, her clothes!"

"And you," Desmond said, distastefully.

"What do you expect?" Maggie flared.

"I'll call Keith," Desmond said, pulling out his mobile phone.

"Why don't you just come in, and help me, Mr Marsden?"

"I can't go in there!" Desmond said, looking mortified.

"Why not? Nobody else can at the moment."

"David will go in and help, won't you, David?" Desmond said, coaxingly.

"David's got a bad back. He can't go in there," Maggie said. "Sit down, David. You'll make things worse."

"I'm not going into the ladies' lavatory!" Desmond asserted, spitting out the words between his teeth, and proceeding with the call.

At least two other women tried to get into the lavatory while Desmond was talking to Keith on the phone. A knot of women customers, who wished to relieve themselves, had gathered outside the door, and a waitress was listening sympathetically to their complaints. They had called the manager.

The manager did not appear to be so generous when he swayed over to Desmond's table this time. But eventually he accepted Desmond's assurance that a team from the Hall would arrive in moments. They would, Desmond said, clean and disinfect the place like a hospital. While Desmond agonised, anxious women waited, or reluctantly climbed the stairs. Tempers simmered. Keith, true to form, arrived in half an hour with two female carers, fresh nappies, towels, cleaning materials, powders and disinfectants, and clean clothes for Cathy. He was business-like and cool, as though this kind of call-out was perfectly ordinary.

Keith returned a refurbished and cheerful Cathy, to them twenty minutes after his ministrations began.

"She's been having a whale of a time in the loo, haven't you, darling?" he said.

Keith's squad disappeared very quickly, and Desmond's small procession wound its way towards the front door. Desmond, in the lead, seemed to dissociate himself, while Cathy, with help from Maggie and David, proceeded with her leg-locked gait like

47

a walking peg. Customers of the White Swan glanced up from their beers, and probably thought Cathy was drunk, until they saw Maggie in her blue check shirt, with a plastic photo-identity card on a cord around her neck. Then they looked away.

David spent a few mornings wandering about the Eccleston Street area, hoping to see somebody exercising Poppy, other than Mrs Temple. One day, Poppy was collected by a man in a van, which was full of dogs. Poppy was quickly bundled inside, and the van drove off in the direction of the South Downs. If that was the regular arrangement for Poppy, then David thought his mission was hopeless.

On another morning, Poppy was collected by a stout, elderly woman with a mop of silver curls, who had four other dogs on leashes at the same time. One dog was a German Shepherd, another a woolly Old English Sheepdog with hair over its eyes, and two small well-barbered poodles. Mrs Temple's maid, alarmed by the barking and scrambling of the animals on the porch, dropped Poppy's leash before the dog-woman could grasp it. The maid bolted back inside the door, and shut it quickly, and the dog-walker had to dive into the melee of animals to retrieve the leash.

The dog-walker had a rich round voice, commanding 'Justina' to come to heel. She soon assumed control of Poppy, and quietened the rest of the pack, issuing grave threats to Adolf, the shepherd, and Hercules, the sheepdog.

The dog-walker progressed slowly down Eccleston Street, drawn by the straining animals, talking to the dogs in firm clear tones, about what was in store for them in the way of food, a bath, and grooming, and asserting how they would love it.

"You're all thoroughly spoiled, you lot," she said to them.

At times, she commented to the dogs on what took her fancy in the street.

"That's a delightful basket of lobelia, Hercules. That wonderful misty purple-white effect."

David was moving hesitantly under the trees, near the opposite side of the street, and deciding that he must take this opportunity. He swayed across the road.

"Excuse me, could I speak to you, please?"

The dog-woman watched his approach. She stopped, ringed by her charges. She had the haughty look of a celebrity surrounded by bodyguards.

"L-l-l-ovely dogs," David said.

Before the woman could reply, Poppy began to bark, and strain at the leash.

"Quiet, Justina!"

Poppy was powerful enough to pull the woman toward him. At this moment, Adolf too, began to bark and strain. The poodles started yapping, and Hercules, who had watched with his one visible blue eye, joined in. David was engulfed by a pack of yelping dogs, pawing at him, and got caught up in their leashes.

The commanding shouts of the dog-walker could not restore order, but she held the leashes firmly. David was able to extricate himself, soiled and a little frightened, with a small tear in his trousers from the teeth of one of the poodles. He was unhurt. As the dogs began to quieten down under the woman's orders, David fell back several feet beyond their radius.

"Whew! I...th-thought..." he began.

"You're all right, of course, young man! Soft as butter. That's what they are. Soft as butter!"

"L-l-l-ovely dogs," he said again, as the woman began to proceed on her way, impregnable within the cordon of her guards.

"They're very boisterous," she said lightly, turning her head back to David with her chin up, "and you have to keep clear, even if you love them!"

8

When the White Swan became too difficult, David continued to take Cathy for visits to Cafe Nero in Brighton, or 'Fay Nero' as she called it, for cappuccino and chocolate cake – that was if he could arrange the Hall's minibus. He would spoon broken pieces of cake into Cathy's mouth, and lift the cup to her lips. When Cathy didn't swallow, chocolate and cream dripped from her chin. He would end their treat with a pile of crumpled paper napkins in front of him on the table. The lower part of Cathy's carefully wiped face, would have a distinct brown tinge. They both enjoyed themselves, but these occasions became less and less possible as the months passed. Now Cathy could not walk, talk or perform any task. Her limbs had become uncontrollable flippers, and she was fed and pottied like a baby. Through this deterioration she retained a sedateness and sense of humour, which David admired. Cathy could still sometimes understand a joke, and she still laughed.

The mystery about Cathy, was how much she understood about what was happening around her. Clearly, an ever-diminishing *something*, but exactly how much? Cathy was viewed with affection by the staff, but did they, nevertheless, have to take care what they said about her, in her presence? This unknown set Cathy apart – the increasingly useless body, locking in a mind which was much less useless. Not everybody dealing with Cathy reckoned on the probability that she knew more than her bodily signals suggested.

Desmond was the prime example. After Cathy had been at the Hall a couple of years, he spoke in front of her as though she wasn't there. The staff were much more sensitive, but David could see a point, not too far ahead, when Cathy would become merely part of the furniture.

Before Cathy's ability to speak had declined markedly, she tried to explain her condition to David. He remembered a summer, when he was wheeling her along the Brighton esplanade. The Denby Hall minibus, which had transported a group of inmates to the beach, was parked a quarter of a mile back. Cathy and David had Ian's permission to go off for half an hour on their own, while the rest of the group sat in deck chairs in the sun and licked ice-creams. David pushed Cathy along the footpath and cycle track, past the bathing huts and the sunburnt croquet green. He stopped in a bus shelter to rest his painful leg, pulling the wheelchair close. He took a cigarette from the supply he carried for Cathy, lit it, and held it to her lips. The noise from the passing cars and buses was partially shielded by the shelter. No other people were on the footpath at that time. They were quite private.

Cathy drew deeply on the cigarette. She was regretting the scene she had made a little earlier, in the confusion, when they were getting off the bus.

"I know I get frustrated, and I start shouting when I can't get what I want."

"Nobody cares. A bit of noise."

"I can sometimes understand what's going on, but I can't communicate what I want, David."

"You're doing well."

"You sound like Dr Floor. I'm conscious. I know what's going on in my mind. I understand a lot of what's going on in the minds of others. But there's a gulf, a disconnection. I can be manipulated, but I can't manipulate."

David grinned. "People ask questions we can't answer,

and then they act on the answers they've supplied themselves."

"I can't do anything but cry out. You see, it's like being bricked into a cell."

"Prison?"

"Yes. The cell has a solid roof and walls. There's no door. I can't get out. I'll never get out. And the bricks are constantly being added to the small viewing space I have."

"You can see through the hole," David said, optimistically.

Cathy was being pragmatic, not looking for sympathy. She talked as though she was describing a piece of building work.

"I can more or less *see and hear* who is out there, through the hole, but they can't really hear me – except you – although sometimes they think they can. I have to scream."

"What about the bricks?" David asked.

"As more bricks are placed in the space where the hole is, the view diminishes. Everything is gradually disappearing from view. I can see, hear and feel less. I'm being buried alive, bricked into a dark cavity. Eventually, only a tiny crack of light will come in, if that."

Cathy was calmly serious.

David was disturbed. "Who… places the bricks?"

Cathy's face smoothed. "Nobody in particular, although I suppose people's actions sometimes cause more bricks to be placed. It's part of the process, I guess."

"Process?"

"Dying. The progress of the disease."

"Can I do anything?"

"Nobody can do anything. I'm reconciled to the dying of the light. It's all right. It's what's happening to me. I've got used to the idea. It's almost comforting to distance myself from what's happening out there. I'm a very sick person, David. And when I say 'I', I don't have any sense of myself. I can't find myself."

"I'm not sure I can either. Maybe I lost myself in the accident. Maybe I never found myself anyway," David said.

"The truth, David, I think, is that there's no self to find. All there is, is a bunch of reflexes and responses, coordinated in different ways at different times. When people say, 'This is Cathy,' or, pointing to the past, say 'That was Cathy' it's an illusion. It's an illusion in the sense that it's not constant. It's always changing, depending upon who sees what, at that moment. It's a great freedom to find that there's no definitive self. I can give up the search…"

"Do you think that's why people shy away from us… because we've kind of become disembodied or …disintegrated?"

"I don't think we've disintegrated, because we were never together. Nor were other people ever together. No. Others can still see what they *regard* as me, my body, like the gnarled old trunk of a tree, which survives the falling of leaves and branches over the years. But that old tree-trunk isn't me. This useless body isn't me."

David had a view of Cathy as a spirit, free of her body. "What are you, then?"

"I think…I'm just a consciousness, in an ever-thickening darkness."

David found the thought pleasing. He, too, was a consciousness in cloudy daylight.

Cathy said, "I'll tell you what I do. I close my eyes. I don't breathe. I let my breath come when it comes. If worries or fears come, I let them go, let them drift away. I feel there is nothing I want to grasp. It's all empty, and I'm empty. I have no sense of 'self' at all. I have let go and I'm at rest, completely free."

Cathy's face was suffused in a smile, her eyes shone with changing lights, and her long, thin, dark eyebrows puckered. David fussed with the wheelchair, releasing the wheel-brakes. He tucked the cigarettes and matches into his pocket.

Cathy strained back to see him. She had an impish look.

She shrugged, and said quietly, "You see, what's happening to me is both fearful, and liberating at the same time."

David patted her arm, and began to wheel the chair back along the promenade, toward the Denby Hall minibus. The sun was warm, and David felt like having a vanilla ice-cream.

After David had been at Denby Hall for more than a year, his father came on a visit, a little put out that David had neither telephoned nor come home for a weekend recently. They ended the visit, after a short walk, in the empty sitting room. They were surrounded by the old collection of beaten up musical instruments used by the music class; the stained drums, dented trumpets and guitars with three strings. The sun streamed in on the faded couch. The room was very hot.

His father set his jaw seriously, and assumed a lower, more intimate tone. "I know you've had a bad knock, son, but the doctors tell me that your intelligence is unimpaired. You're a very clever boy. You can't remember the past at the moment, but there's no limit to what you can achieve in the present and future. No limit."

"That's good, but I'm not sure what I want to do."

"I just want you to remember, David, that you can't mark time here at Denby Hall."

"Why not?"

"The future!" his father said, opening his eyes wide.

"What is that?" David asked cautiously.

"David, it's a long road, fraught with challenges, and obstacles to be overcome."

"If that's what it is, I'm not sure I want to go there."

His father disregarded the comment. He said, as though it was a revelation, "You have to have a plan."

"Supposing I don't have a plan ... can't make up my mind?"

"No such thing as can't! I'm here to help."

"Can it be *my* plan?"

This request surprised his father

"As long as you're serious, David," he said doubtfully. "You have to be serious."

It was difficult, perhaps impossible, to explain to his father and Caroline, that the future for him was his next step in the sunlight. It was not hard to say this, but it was hard to get them to understand what he meant.

9

David was disappointed with his efforts to beguile the dog-walker, but he decided to have one last try, anticipating that Mrs Temple might have a variety of arrangements for a daily task that was expensive. He chose a fine Saturday morning, and made his way to Eccleston Street after breakfast. He waited, and watched on the other side of the street, in the shadow of the trees. At about ten am, a young girl in her teens pushed the buzzer on the door of number 73. In a few moments, the maid brought Poppy outside onto the porch, and handed over the leash.

David kept well away from the girl, as she was tugged down Eccleston Street by Poppy. He was optimistic at what he had seen. He thought he couldn't get anyone easier to deal with than a young girl on her own, or anyone who was as likely to be sympathetic to his request. He had an idea that she would head for the public park and football fields which were, like Denby Hall, at the edge of the housing development. It was the only suitable place in the vicinity, and many people walked their dogs there. David followed discreetly as she took this direction.

The park and football fields were a vast space of neatly mown, blindingly green grass, which curved up a slope in the distance to a plantation of pine trees. Apart from the girl and Poppy, and one distant man and his dog, the area was deserted. The girl let Poppy off the leash. The dog dashed round in wide circles, jumping and stretching her muscles. The girl did her best to race alongside.

It was an ideal opportunity for David to speak to her. He began to limp across the field. Poppy saw him when he was fifty yards away. The dog stopped, took a second to make sure it was him, and ran towards him at full speed, yowling. When Poppy reached David, she sprang up, almost knocking him over.

The girl was alarmed by Poppy's sudden reaction. She ran towards David, calling "Justina, Justina!"

David laughed when the girl came up, and said, "It's OK... she's just being friendly."

He patted Poppy, and slapped her flanks, and she turned around him, bouncing with affection. The girl came closer, and when Poppy was near her she grasped Poppy's collar and clipped on the leash.

"I'm terribly, terribly sorry!" she said.

"She knows me... It's all right."

"Really?" the girl said, looking relieved. "I thought for one horrible moment she was attacking you. I don't know what I'd do if that happened!"

"She wouldn't do that. She used to be owned by a friend of mine at Denby Hall."

"Denby Hall?"

The girl looked serious. She knew about Denby Hall.

"Yes, Cathy Marsden. I've walked Poppy a lot. 'Poppy' is what Cathy calls her."

"I see," the girl said cautiously. "I'm glad you're not hurt. I'll have to go," she added, pulling Poppy away.

"Look...can I talk to you a moment?"

The girl's soft, pale face stiffened, and she drew back further, trying to still the restless Poppy.

"I think I saw you in Eccleston Street, earlier," the girl said, with a hint of suspicion.

She was working out that this wasn't a casual encounter.

"Could we take Poppy ... Justina to Denby Hall?" David

said, realising as he said it, how bald, and unpalatable it sounded.

The girl, testing her strength against Poppy as she tried to retreat, said, "No, why? Of course not!"

"I mean, only to see Cathy for maybe half an hour."

"I don't know you. It's Mrs Temple's dog," she said, shrilly.

"Poppy used to be Cathy's dog," David replied, the words tripping over themselves weakly, as his confidence evaporated.

The girl shook her head in disagreement, backing away pulling Poppy with her, but Poppy easily pulled back to David, wrinkling her nose with pleasure. He bent over and wiggled Poppy's soft ears. He was aware that he could take Poppy if he called her, but also aware that such a step would only create more problems.

"Please!" the girl cried out, "Please let Justina go!"

The girl's fear was like a virus which drained his strength. He had an explanation, if only he could start over again, but it was beyond his ability, at that instant, to get the words, and the ideas, in the right order.

"Please let me take her back!" the girl said, her voice rising in alarm.

David became conscious that the man he had seen in the distance exercising his dog was bearing down upon them at a run. He was a heavy man, in a blue track-suit with bristly grey hair. His dog, an old Scots' terrier, was trying to keep up.

The man, sweating and red, shouted to the girl from ten yards, "Is this guy bothering you?"

"He's trying to take my dog," the girl cried, turning to the man thankfully.

"I thought something was up. From way over there. Body language!"

"He's from Denby Hall," she said.

"The nut-house?"

The man looked closely at David, and saw a plump, soft looking, uncertain sort of person. His aggression lessened slightly.

"I'd beat it, son. Back to where you come from. And don't get any ideas about girls walkin' round here. You oughta be locked up. Go on, scram!"

David wanted to tell the girl that he didn't mean to frighten her, but the man was standing in front of her, blocking her out, and the words wouldn't come. Poppy was whimpering.

David turned his back on them, and made a slow path across the empty green.

David was sitting in his room, watching television one afternoon, when he heard Cathy start up like a siren. Loud, deep cries of frustration were coming down the corridor. He knew that Cathy had been visited that day, by an official from one of the health authorities, or social security departments. There were so many of these departments with a finger in the pudding that David was at a loss to know who was responsible for what, even in his own case. He supposed that Cathy's case was no different. He had heard from Rose that an official wanted to come and see Cathy. David had learned that officials never came to ask; they came to tell, if they said anything at all. Cathy's fear was that 'they' wanted to move her to another home.

David went down the corridor to Cathy's room. It was a bright place, with wide windows, looking out over the row of apartments across the road. Beyond, were rolling hills, studded thickly with houses. The dresser and bedtable were cluttered with greetings cards, and postcards, mostly old, and curling in the sun. There were family photographs, some in blackened silver frames, photographs of healthy children, nephews and nieces who had never appeared at Denby Hall.

On the bed was a cluster of teddy bears, including a very old one that Cathy had had as a child, and another, with patches all over it, called Lucan.

Cathy was in her wheelchair, raging. Keith was bending down to her level, trying to soothe her, and joking as he dodged her swinging arms.

"Don't knock me about, love."

David put his head in the door with an uneasy look.

"The nurse from the local authority upset her," Keith said.

Cathy seemed determined to communicate something to them. She looked furiously from one to the other, waving her fists, choking, as mangled words came out. They couldn't understand what she was saying.

"What's she unhappy about?" David asked.

"I dunno. Not knowing what's going to happen to her? Could be."

"Is she going to leave Denby Hall?"

"I dunno. Depends on the Funders. She's got to have an assessment first, haven't you love?"

David knew about assessments from his own experience, and from his talks with Mark and John. The Funders were a mysterious, amorphous presence, who could materialise in the form of two or three uncommunicative people, with clipboards and notebooks.

David had been visited recently by a pair who arrived at the Hall carrying thick brief-cases. A woman in shapeless dark clothes, with tousled hair, and a man in an anorak, with a long, grey pony tail. They had coffee offered by the staff, and talked with Dr Floor. They were joined by Keith, Maggie, as David's key worker, and Helmut. Helmut, who did not intend to be present at the meeting himself, had insisted to them, in David's presence, that David should sit in at the meeting.

"His father can't get along today," Helmut said, "but the boy can understand, and he ought to hear this."

Muted murmurs of disapproval came from the Funders. "Medical detail could be upsetting ... not the usual practice..."

"Nothing will come up that David hasn't heard already in his many visits to the doctors," Helmut insisted.

Helmut's ingenuous proposal in David's presence defied outright opposition, but the Funders were uncomfortable. Nobody addressed David during the entire meeting, except to show how impressed they were by the talented person he had been.

The officials hunched over their pads and papers, asking each other questions. The drift of talk, as far as David could interpret it, was that in a period of months he would move out of Denby Hall. Arrangements would be made for his further education and training.

David wanted to say, 'Excuse me, but I'm not very interested in learning to work a computer... I don't think I could remember the key sequences. And I don't particularly want to go back to Somerset...' but he couldn't find a place to fit the words, which bubbled in his mind, into the discussion.

When the meeting closed, it was evident that it had been satisfactory. The Funders smiled, stood up, yawned, stretched and accepted another cup of coffee. They turned their backs on David, and talked agreeably with the Denby Hall staff, while they put their papers away. David reflected that it didn't matter that his father wasn't there, because the assessors were, like his father, entirely preoccupied with a tomorrow, which they had constructed in their own minds for him.

David expected that Cathy's assessment, when it came, would follow the same inexorable drift as his own. You couldn't protest; there was nobody to protest to. Everybody agreed with what was happening, except you.

"She doesn't want to leave Denby Hall," David said to Keith.

"Yes, I know, but that doesn't count, David."

"Why?"

"Cathy's too ill to say what she wants, or know what's good for her."

"But she *is* saying."

Keith stopped brushing Cathy's hair for a moment. "You're right, David, yes, in a way. But it still doesn't count. It's a case of what's in her best interests."

"Who knows what they are?"

"The Funders."

"I thought the Funders were trying to save money. That's what Mark, John, and everybody says."

Keith smoothed Cathy's brow, drawing her hair back with a comb, and catching it in a flowery band. "Make you look nice, dear."

He looked sharply at David. "I kid you not, David. They are looking for a cheap way out. It's public money after all."

"But you said the Funders were deciding what was in Cathy's best interests."

David wanted to try to follow this elusive fairy of 'best interests.'

"Well, it's in Cathy's interests, if it's not too expensive."

"What's too expensive?"

Keith threw up his arms. "Search me! Too expensive is what the Funders say it is."

"I thought it was free, if you're very sick."

"David, nothing is free. Not a goddam thing on the planet, let alone health care."

"Mark says the politicians are always talking about a free service."

"If you're very ill, but not actually dying, like say, Cathy, it costs. Depends how much dosh you've got. They milk you."

"But Cathy is very ill …"

"David, what is *very* ill? Say you're dying. OK, dying's free, provided they think you're not going to take too long. Anybody else is out of luck. But it's a nice thought, free care."

"Isn't there a way of telling who is *very* ill?"

"Certainly there is! That's the beauty of the system. Every authority has their own guidelines, measuring instruments and scoring tables. They have ombudsman's rulings, court decisions and directions from the secretary of state. Reams of paper. It's a real bugger's muddle. Nobody can understand it!"

"B-because it's too expensive?"

"Too expensive. And it really is bloody expensive!"

"But if people can't understand …"

"Look, here's the neat way it works. The ordinary punters outside can't understand the test, and everybody inside pretends they can! So it's unchallengeable, you see? You look at the rules, score this, estimate that, throw in a specialist opinion, and a medical report, and you think you've made a case for your granny. But you'll be told there are fifty eight reasons why you're wrong, if you're so lucky as to get an explanation!"

"If what Cathy wants is disregarded … what about her husband?" David asked, trying a different tack.

Keith was anxious to go, and he handed the wheelchair to David, now that Cathy had calmed down, and said, "Take her downstairs. Naah. What Desmond wants doesn't figure."

"Surely…"

"Well, they'll probably listen to Desmond Marsden, if he digs his oar in deep enough, because he's an educated bloke, but that's all. Smartest to listen to an educated bloke first, because he might catch you out."

"So he could stop Cathy going?"

"Doubt it. They listen to the Desmond Marsdens first, then do what they want. Next of kin, David, are viewed like a piece of dog turd in the road."

"Desmond's quite …forceful."

"He only gets to speak if he insists. And all that comes back is the echo."

Keith was only rehearsing what David had already heard from Mark and John, and partly experienced himself. Both Cathy and David were in 'their' hands. David's expectations for Cathy's assessment were low. He feared it would lead to disappointment and departure for her, and the loss of a friend for him. But when Keith had gone, he made a lot of cheery remarks to her and, instead of taking her to the sitting room, they stayed in her room and played the DVD she loved for the umpteenth time; Queen's *Rare Live*.

10

David had seen the photographs in Cathy's room. A few shots of now deceased elderly people. Her mother. Her father, a career soldier, in the army uniform of a brigadier, posed in a flower garden. And a number of people of her own generation, and younger. Desmond was well represented; head and shoulders, with a collar and tie, as a business executive, and with dark glasses on his forehead, in a ski-suit, against a snowy mountainside. Amongst the other prints were her brother and sister, and their children and step-children – a variety of healthy, fresh-faced, smiling people, who never visited Denby Hall.

Although the photographs cluttered Cathy's dresser, bedside table, and window ledge, and seemed to imply affection, David thought of them as a show. Not a show by Cathy, who never referred to them, or spoke about them. They were a show by Desmond, and perhaps the care assistants at the Hall, who wanted to create a family atmosphere.

David liked to try to find out about the photographs. Cathy was not always very explicit. One photograph of Cathy and her sister showed a cottage on a rugged piece of Scottish coast; a holiday cottage in happier times. Another, with Cathy's sister and young children, showed a camp site by a lake. A portrait in a silver frame, had the head and shoulders of Desmond's son by a previous marriage, with his bride. And there was a separate picture of a baby.

The process of family survival was going on relentlessly 'out there'. Desmond's son, according to Cathy, was a tenacious, thrusting, self-made multi-millionaire in his early thirties, who had grown a 'dot com' company. He was providing a regime of comfort, and privilege for his offspring, founding a dynasty which would burgeon like the shoots of a plane tree in spring. David had a sense of the different but connected lives, procreating, and spreading unseen and unknown at Denby Hall, while Cathy, childless, withered away.

The very early part of Cathy's life only became known to David, when a Portugese girl started to work as a care assistant at the Hall. Cathy had two red clay figures, about four inches tall, on a shelf. One was an old man with a fish basket, and the other was an Indian with a long-handled fork. The Portugese girl recognised the figures as Brazilian peasant trinkets. Cathy surprised everybody, by revealing that she could speak Brazilian-Portugese. The pair chattered in two languages about their experiences.

Cathy told David that she had worked for four years for the Volunteer Service Abroad, in Brazil, when she left Edinburgh university. She had a romance with a Brazilian doctor, which she mentioned lingeringly, but otherwise didn't want to talk about. She pointed to a faded bundle of letters in her drawer, the faint echoes of a far distant and inaccessible past. She showed him some photographs of her, with black children, taken in front of reed huts, near Manaus on the Amazon River. She said they had been shot by a roving journalist from the *Sunday Mirror*, and published in that paper, with a story about her self-sacrifice. She jested about being famous for one day.

Cathy said she had returned home from Brazil in her late twenties, to a series of jobs as a community worker on London housing estates. She met Desmond at a charity fund-raising event, when she was in her early thirties. He was a design engineer who had a broken marriage behind him, and a modestly prosperous lifestyle. She wanted to talk about her marriage.

"You're like a priest, David," she said to him, "You just smile and forgive me. And I suppose, what I'm saying about my marriage to Desmond, is a confession. I was attracted to him, but I never really wanted to get married. This is my confession, that I had some inkling of the onset of my illness. Of course I didn't know what it was, and wouldn't for fifteen years. But I knew I wasn't *right*. I never told anybody. I was scared at times, and at other times I thought or hoped it was a passing feeling. I lived with woman-friends, in a leaky, damp apartment in Pimlico. I had little or no savings and I saw that marriage could be a shelter. But I was also afraid that it would bring responsibilities that I couldn't perform.

"Desmond and I lived together for a few months, but I still had my place in Pimlico. I wanted to give it up and live with him on a permanent basis. I got on easily with his two kids. Desmond didn't want any more children. I knew instinctively that I couldn't handle parenthood, and I had myself sterilised. That's an unusual insight for a woman to have. We could have gone on as partners, but Desmond wanted marriage. He said he couldn't go around introducing me to his work colleagues, all the big peas he met, and the children's friends, as his girlfriend or partner. It wasn't done at that time, and Desmond was very conventional. After a few months, Desmond wore me down – he's a persistent, determined man – I caved in, and we married.

"I remember the day, as every bride does. I left work after lunch, and we met at the grotty registry office at Camden Town Hall. Desmond had to go outside on to the street and find two people who were prepared to be witnesses. He persuaded a couple of old pensioners. A few mumblings from the clerk, a quick signing, our thanks to the pensioners with a tenner for them to buy a drink, and we were back on the street. We bought fish and chips. We took them home and ate them out of the paper, with a couple of cans of beer to wash them down.

"As I look back, it was a disastrous day for Desmond, but not for me.

"As you get older you begin to wonder if your brain is failing. You see demented people around you, and you think about yourself. You forget things, lose your concentration, feel sometimes that you're out of your head. I suppose everybody has that experience at times, and ponders about their sanity. As it happened, I *was* going mad. That's how I was beginning to be when I met Desmond, although I tried to hide it. If you had asked me then, I would have said I wasn't being deceptive, I was merely protecting myself against something dark and frightening around the corner, which I hoped wasn't even really there.

"At first, the doctors diagnosed me as a depressive. That diagnosis held good for years. I just couldn't cope with the world making its jarring and grinding changes around me, and I had to stop work and go to bed. Once, when we were in Canada on holiday, I spent just about the whole time, at every hotel where we stayed, in bed. I had drugs which made me sleep day and night.

"Desmond's attitude was superficially kind, but he really thought that I was a weakling who wouldn't make an effort. He thought, although he didn't say, that what had happened to me was my *fault*, and I could shake it off, if I only had the will.

"One day, a specialist who was treating me for a minor rheumatic ailment, noticed something odd in my walk, as I crossed his surgery. He said, 'You have a movement problem, and you ought to have a brain-scan.' I didn't think I had a movement problem, and I had never thought of a brain scan. Desmond insisted on the scan.

"I remember going to another consultant's rooms in Harley Street with Desmond to get the result. The place was gloomy, hung with heavy drapes. Very little light could get in the windows. The smell was of depression and death, which I suppose is what they dealt with there. We spent a long time, speechless, with a couple of other silent people, in a tiny, dark waiting room. We were sitting so close to them, that we could share their misery without a word being spoken.

"When we were summoned, the consultant was sitting in a high backed chair, a broad table width away from us. Behind him was a bookshelf crowded with faded blue and red volumes. Before him, an untidy expanse of old manila files. He was bald, with a pimply, flacid face. We crouched awkwardly on our chairs. The consultant made the terse announcement, that the film showed that my brain had deteriorated. He said that there was no special name for the condition. It was 'non-specific cerebral degeneration', and it was irreversible. He was quite brutal about it.

'Is there any medication or treatment that will help?' Desmond asked him.

'Come back in twenty years,' the consultant said.

"Yes, that's what he said. He seemed to be watching us to see the effect of his words. In his irony there was a tinge of masochism. We didn't cry, or sob. We were both stunned.

"As we were leaving, the consultant said, 'You better take this, you paid for it.'

"He handed Desmond a cardboard envelope about two feet square. It contained the film of my brain.

"Desmond took me to a coffee shop around the corner in Cavendish Street. We sat at a tiny table on the pavement, with the traffic roaring and fuming around us, and pedestrians pushing past. I was trying to drink scalding cappuccino, and trying to make sense of what we had been told: my brain had actually started to deteriorate, like a rotten cabbage.

'I could have punched his face, the arrogant bastard,' Desmond said.

"But a new era had dawned. At least my condition wasn't my fault any longer. Much later Desmond took me to a neurologist who insisted on a diagnosis. He concluded it was Huntington's disease, and a blood test showed this to be true.

"You see what Desmond's conventional attitudes got him into, David? If we had remained friends, I would guess that Desmond would have lost patience with my continual 'depression', and, feeling less obligation, would have left me, years before events came to a conclusion in the brain scan. But we were man and wife, and he stuck it out."

While the residents were at lunch, Poppy appeared on the porch, and sat watching, moving her head from one side to the other every few moments, to catch a glimpse through the glass. At this time, John Murdoch, a resident who, like David, could go out alone by arrangement, arrived home after a walk. John considered himself an expert on Labradors. He had already noted Poppy's finer points to some of the other residents and staff. He explained that she was a retriever, a powerful sports dog, by breeding. He said she was probably the product of two black parents, carrying a golden gene. Whether this was a fact or not, the idea of two black Labradors having a gorgeous golden puppy, fascinated his listeners.

John stopped to pat Poppy, and talk to her, then pressed the entry buzzer. When Kay unlocked and opened the door, Poppy moved first and rushed inside, her thrust defying any attempt to close the door on her.

John laughed and Kay, who had been caught out by Poppy's speed, held her hands to her head in consternation. Kay had been specifically instructed by both the shift managers that Poppy was not allowed inside.

"What will I do?" she said.

Poppy paused briefly in the deserted lobby, moving her muzzle about sensitively.

"Don't worry. A welcome guest!" John said.

"Keith will kill me!" Kay said.

Poppy disappeared in the direction of the dining room, which was signalled by a babble of voices, the tinkle of knives and forks, and a warm broccoli smell.

Poppy entered the dining room with three deafening, chesty barks. The usual clamour subsided quickly. Poppy had gained complete attention. When she saw Cathy in her wheelchair, drawn up alongside the table shared with David and Mark, Poppy ran to her. She darted between care assistants who were serving the meal, and knocked one aside, causing her to drop her plates.

The dog reared up and rested her forepaws in Cathy's lap. Poppy was lithe, probably five years old, and thirty kilos in weight. The impetus of her rush swung Cathy's wheelchair, which was supposed to be braked, against the flimsy table, and upset the table with a crash. Mark and David tumbled backwards, and nearly fell off their chairs.

All those who could stand were on their feet, the food forgotten. Tables and chairs were pushed hurriedly and noisily out of the way, sending dishes and cutlery clattering to the floor. Residents who could operate their own wheelchairs, spun them around like dodgems, to get a better view of the spectacle.

Everybody was cheering, and waving. Barney Colas jumped on a table, and started to throw handfuls of potato salad over the heads of the crowd. Seeing this, Ted Kelsey, a

71

muscular man with tattoos on his bare forearms, leaped upon another table. Under the impact of his hornpipe dance, it collapsed on the floor, making a loud explosion. Ted brought down two other residents in his fall.

Poppy and Cathy seemed to know they were the subject of the hubbub. Poppy remained with her paws in Cathy's lap, and let out some friendly barks. Cathy raised one clenched fist and cried, "Arrrrrrgh!" as the occupants of the room pressed around them.

"Stop, stop, stop!"

An unlikely stentorian roar from Helmut penetrated the hilarity.

The shouts and laughter dried up. Even Poppy resumed her four legs, and looked shamefacedly around at Helmut. He stood on a chair by the door. The residents who had fallen, picked themselves up with quiet help from the care assistants.

Helmut's voice was as stern and guttural as they had ever heard it.

"We cannot haff this! Now you understand why a dog is not allowed!"

11

The garden, and the cliff path, had a desolation which encouraged both Cathy and Desmond to share their more serious thoughts with David. The atmosphere inside Denby Hall was different. David could not imagine what they said, being said inside the Hall. Cathy's bedroom had dolls, and tinsel stars; in the sitting room, in front of the battered piano, there was a resonance of sing-songs; but in the garden, under the tortured branches of the pines, or on the cliff, with the sea crawling away to the horizon, intimate thoughts claimed their place. In the time when she could speak, Cathy told David of the shock of her diagnosis.

"I felt certainty at last. Instead of sliding into a deep pit, not knowing how far down I would go, or what agony would beset me at its lowest point, I had a definite path. Awful, yes, but definite. I would lose the ability to speak, I would lose the power in my limbs, my body would jerk convulsively. My scope of space would reduce, until the last brick was placed in the wall of my cell.

"It must seem difficult to believe that I could be – am – resigned about such a fate. But that resignation isn't so unusual. Think of the people you know who have had grave illnesses. They don't rave, and fret, and curse the stars, do they? Once you know where you're going, *where you have to go*, there is acceptance. Now, the plight of the living – who also have to endure this disease – is quite different from that of the dying.

"When Desmond had to tell the family that the tests showed I had Huntington's of course they were shocked. If one of your parents has the gene, you have a fifty-fifty chance of getting it. I had no idea that one of my parents carried the gene, but they must have. My discovery was also a ghastly suspended sentence on my brother and sister, who were equally ignorant. And it was a suspended sentence on their kids. A guillotine, might, or might not, drop on one or all of them.

"Simon and Denise had to face the blood test, or stick their heads in the sand. If they had the test, they might be in the clear, and they could forget the disease as far as their children were concerned. If they didn't have the test, they would never know, and would have to live with a dreadful possibility, which they might see worked out in madness in themselves, or their own children or grandchildren.

"The family looked at the family tree as far as they knew it, perhaps seeking somebody to 'blame.' But they could find no evidence, or anecdote, from the living or the dead about the disease. My forbears must have been very skilful in covering what they probably perceived as the stigma of madness. But that's what people do, David. They cover up madness. There are a lot of Mrs Rochesters around.

"Even now, I'm not clear whether some of my nephews and nieces know what has happened to me. People are awfully nervous about admitting, even within the family, that somebody in the family is mad. I know that my sister, Denise, got very upset with Desmond when he spoke, I think innocently, to one of her children. Desmond told me that his conversation with Stuart seemed to be the emotional equivalent of exploding a grenade at Denise's breakfast table. She has two bright kids, Stuart and Jennifer, one in the oil industry, and the other in publishing. I used to keep in touch with them. A dutiful aunt, remembering their birthdays over many years. I wonder what my sister said when they asked, 'Whatever happened to Auntie Cathy?'

"She's a good mother in many ways, Denise. A divorced single mother. Her husband left her for another woman. She's also rather neurotic. Your confidence takes a dive when your husband walks out on you. I understand her. I love her. She just can't bear to face what I am. I don't expect a visit. I know she loves me. She probably lies awake at night on occasions, shedding tears for me – and herself. She simply can't face it."

Desmond, in one of his many monologues to David on the cliff path, had described graphically the telephone call he received from Denise about six months after he told her, and Cathy's brother, of Cathy's diagnosis.

"The call came at an unsocial hour," he said, "About ten-thirty at night. I was at home alone, reading in bed. I could tell, as soon as I picked up the receiver, that the person at other end was charged with emotion. Her breath was coming in rasping gulps and her words were falling over themselves. She didn't announce who she was.

'You are a real shit of the first order, Desmond, a lousy, low shit! You've interfered in my life with your vile ideas, and you've just about wrecked my family…' she sobbed.

'Hang on, Denise.'

'Don't try to say you don't know what I'm talking about! You've talked to Stuart.'

'Yes, I talked to Stuart.'

'How dare you!'

' I didn't know what he didn't know, Denise.'

'How dare you *assume* he knew about Cathy, without talking to me first?"

'I never assumed anything. I met Stuart completely by chance. I had a business meeting at his office, with other people. Afterwards, we talked …'

'Don't try to weasel out! You interfered in the most delicate matter between my son and me … God! A matter of life and death!'

'Stuart asked me about Cathy. I said it was helpful to have the Huntington's diagnosis. He asked a few questions about Huntington's. I gave the answers. That's all. He never let on that he didn't know the effect it could have on him.'

'He didn't *know* that Cathy had Huntington's – at that point!' Denise yelled.

'Well, you should have told him months ago.'

'No, you should have buttoned your big mouth! It's my duty as his parent to decide whether, and when to tell him.'

'That's boloney, Denise. Stuart's a man. He's over twenty-one. He's not a little child under your control.'

'It's our family business. It's not for you to stick your nose in.'

'Stuart and Jennifer are *entitled* to know,' Desmond said, in a derisive tone.

'It's my decision whether to tell them.'

'Holding the power of life or death over them – and their children? Come on, Denise.'

'Don't tell me what to do and think, you interfering shit!'

'Look, if you have the test there's a fifty-fifty chance you're in the clear – and then Stuart and Jennifer could be clear without any test.'

'Yes, and there's equally a fifty-fifty chance I'll find out *I have to live in misery*, waiting for the disease to happen!' she screamed.

'You'd rather live with the uncertainty of whether you have the gene or not, for the rest of your life, when you could be worrying about nothing?'

'Don't I have to balance that, with the horror of certainty, if I'm carrying the gene? It's all right for you, you're a spectator. It's my decision!'

'Spectator isn't quite the right word. The gene has screwed up my life too.'

'Not as badly as it could screw up mine.'

'It's not only you, Denise.'

'I'll never forgive you for interfering in our lives!' she shouted, as she slammed down the receiver.

"That's my sister-in-law, David. Lovely woman! I still don't know whether she's roasting on the griddle of uncertainty. And her poor kids, do they know what could be in store for them?"

A lot of Caroline's questions were focussed on David's past, for which she used the simile of a broken stained glass window. She returned to the image over and over again. She said the fragments of glass were mostly gone. Of those that remained in the intricate lead frame, some few pieces were interlinked, clear and bright. Others were isolated, meaningless chips.

"If we work on it David, we can find all the chips, and put the broken pane together," she urged hopefully.

He didn't reply, and she waited. "What's the matter? You don't agree?"

"I don't think there's a lot of different coloured pieces of glass. There's just …nothing."

"Isn't it worth thinking in those terms … and trying?"

He said yes, but it was Caroline who tried to put the pieces of glass from the broken pane together herself, without success. She talked at large to him about his school and academy work, and his former friends and class-mates. She had copious notes, and must have compiled a detailed biography. David's relatives, except his father, could not have been much help in this. His mother was dead, and he was an only child, but Caroline was very well informed.

"Don't you feel any attachment or attraction to the past, David?"

The truth was he felt rather free in not having a past. Both Cathy and Desmond had talked to him about their past, and for him, that was an interesting story to study. Having a past he thought, might be a burden. His past lead in a direction which he could not now go, whether he wanted to or not.

"Do you want to recall it?" Caroline pressed.

"Well, in the sense that it's something everybody has, yes. But I don't really miss it."

"Do you feel that something of value has been lost?"

"No, what has been lost is the future I could have had."

"You can still have a marvellous future," Caroline insisted.

"A different one."

Caroline fidgeted at the lack of progress in her work as a jig-saw puzzle expert, and a glazier. Despite her unease, David was happy to regard his past as mostly closed, and the future…well, that too was a problem, but not to him.

12

Desmond told David he wanted to see Dr Floor about Cathy's assessment. David had put together things he had learned from a number of people over a few months, remarks by Helmut, Rose, Ian and Keith which indicated that Desmond was putting pressure on the authorities to get Cathy moved to a home in London. David took a chance, although it was none of his business, and asked Desmond why Cathy should be moved.

"How did you know she was going to be moved?"

"I thought that's what you wanted."

"Well, I do, but I haven't spoken about it."

Desmond said this in a clipped tone, which was equivalent to 'mind your own business'.

"No, but I've heard whispers ... Cathy's happy here ...why move her?"

Desmond looked at David as though he was being impertinent, but David felt no regret or embarrassment. He had found that the politeness, and courtesies, of people 'out there' were often buttresses for their odd positions.

"A move will be in Cathy's best interests," Desmond said moderately, perhaps considering that David was close enough to Cathy, to have some standing in such intimate matters.

It was the mirage of 'best interests' again.

"Who knows what Cathy's best interests are?" David went on quietly.

"I bloody well do! I'll tell you that!" Desmond exploded, ending the dialogue.

It was always difficult to locate Dr Floor, and so many of the sightings of him proved to be false. He was said to be in the dispensary, only to have disappeared to Room 28, and from there to a meeting in his office, or probably a visit to Room 19. Desmond chased around the building in frustration, the doctor only minutes ahead of him. Dr Floor had always gone a few moments before Desmond arrived. The doctor probably did not know of the pursuit, but his evasion created the annoying suspicion that it must be deliberate.

Dr Floor was jolly in his manner. His face came forward to a beak-like nose. He looked like a rooster, with grey hair standing up stiffly on his forehead in a comb. He appeared to be examining you from two different directions, with an eye on each side of his head. He also had a habit of looking over your shoulder after a few moments, like a guest at a party wanting to move on. Fortunately, Desmond met and accosted Dr Floor in the corridor, when David and Desmond were taking Cathy up to her room.

"Excuse me, Doctor, Desmond Marsden."

"Remember you well, Sir," Dr Floor said, bending down toward Cathy, and patting her arm.

"Could I speak to you about Cathy for a moment?"

"I'm just on my way to…"

"I've left several phone messages for you, ever since my previous visit."

"Sorry. Never get to the phone."

"There's going to be an assessment."

"Indeed. We'll be ready."

"I'd like to know how Cathy is."

"As well as can be expected."

"I'd like to see Cathy's medical report."

"Don't worry."

"But the report…"

"No need. She's fine, bearing in mind..."

"Doctor, I want to see the actual written report."

"Ah, the *written* report?"

Dr Floor examined Desmond from two directions. "Don't trouble yourself."

"Yes. I'm her next of kin, after all."

"Cathy's lucky to have your interest," Dr Floor said, easing past, looking ahead along the length of the empty corridor.

"The report, Doctor. You're doing examinations, and sending updates to the Funders."

"Yes. It's all under control."

"Is there a problem about seeing the document?"

"I wouldn't say that," Dr Floor said, backing away, but forced to retain eye contact by Desmond's intensity.

"What *would* you say?"

"Well... It's not the usual practice."

"Why?"

"Please don't ask me, Mr Marsden. I don't make the rules."

"Where is the rule written?"

"I'm not sure," Dr Floor admitted cheerily, now backed off to six feet.

"I'm Cathy's next of kin, for God's sake. I'm as responsible for her as anybody on this earth."

"It's the Funders' responsibility. We keep them informed."

"Sod the Funders!"

"Why don't you ask them. I'm sure they'll help."

"They're about as forthcoming as a stone bust of the Emperor Augustus!"

"Oh dear. Try them again. Sorry. Must go," Dr Floor said, poised for flight.

"Doctor, I'm a funder too. And Cathy is. We are: a considerable sum every month."

"Funding isn't my department."

"Why can't we be *consulted*?"

"Funders," Dr Floor said, as he fled with a beaky rictus.

Desmond, mumbling imprecations against Dr Floor, and the medical profession, moved towards Cathy's room.

Keith came breezing towards them. "Having a nice time?"

"No!" Desmond said, and he went on to explain the conversation with Dr Floor.

"Oh, yeah. The medicos don't like to pin themselves down, especially in writing."

"Are they afraid?"

"They might make a mistake. You know, a loose word here or there. Bingo! There's a complaint, or a lawsuit. They get reprimanded, maybe suspended. Lose their job."

"I thought we'd got beyond the prerogative of the high priests of Hippocrates to withhold information about a patient."

"Well, yeees, we have, but only in a way. With gravely disabled people like Cathy, obviously she's out of circulation. That leaves the doctors and the Funders. It's a love-in between them, money for treatment. You don't get in here, because you're only next of kin."

"But *why*, Keith? Why don't I get in?"

Keith looked at threads of the carpet, and stirred them with the toe of his shoe. "How can I put it? Patients are a doddle to look after. Mostly they're grateful, and do as they're told. But 'NOK' are quite different, always whining and whingeing, criticising, arguing, complaining. NOK are bad news."

"There's plenty to complain about!"

"Exactly. The doctors get nervous about aiming at two targets at the same time, Funders *and* next of kin. Look at it their way. Imagine having all those rude, ignorant next of kin criticising medical reports, wanting second opinions about treatment, demanding more information, arguing about expenditures, and generally messing up the money for treatment deal that's been worked out with the Funders? Imagine that. Hence you don't get to see the reports. You get a lot of warm, soapy water about how well Cathy is doing."

"But they must know I'm entitled to see the reports."

"Of course they do! But they rely on the ignorance of Joe Public. They push you around. That way they have their ass well covered, and an easier life. "

13

After the debacle in the dining room with Poppy, which the residents viewed as a fine entertainment, David slipped out of the room with Poppy, hitched a cord to her collar, took half an hour's leave, and asked Kay to let him out. He walked down the cliff path, further out of town. He let Poppy off the leash, but she insisted on following him back to the Hall as usual. She sat on the porch for a while, and nobody inside the Hall ventured out to catch her; they were too busy. Then she disappeared.

David went out again that evening and fed Poppy, after Sally had carved a generous helping of raw beef from one of the joints she was preparing to cook. The next day, Poppy appeared when Cathy and David were in the garden, and they went for a walk together. He fed Poppy later, and they were also able to walk again the following day. But in the afternoon, Helmut told David that Mrs Temple was coming to the Hall with a complaint about him, and that he should be 'available'.

Mrs Temple arrived by appointment to see Helmut. David was waiting with Helmut in the lobby at the time. They both watched Mrs Temple's large, silver saloon car nose up the drive, as she tried to find a place to park. Staff and service vehicles were tucked in beside the pathway. There was no space. Mrs Temple's search ended with her car blocking the driveway, lodged in a narrow, and slightly twisting defile, between the other vehicles.

"Oh, dear, David. She iss in trouble," Helmut said, grimly.

"Can you help her?"

"I don't think so. She looks very competent."

"She might scratch her car," David said.

"That would be the end!" Helmut said, and he fumbled with the key pad on the door in his anxiety, and let himself out.

David saw Helmut pause to compose himself at the edge of the porch. He approached the car with a relaxed stride, and bent down to the driver's window in a cordial way. David could not hear what was said, but Helmut's offer of help was apparently accepted, and he began to wave Mrs Temple in reverse – the only possibility at this point. Only then did David have a slight doubt about Helmut's capability to do what he was proposing. His gestures of direction were confusing. Helmut, who drove a small, scarred Ford, had the reputation of being an absent minded, and slapdash driver. His skills at parking might have been just as limited.

Mrs Temple moved the car slowly backwards, bouncing around in her seat, looking from the rear-view mirrors to Helmut's varied signals. The narrow lane was treacherous. The gleaming wings of the car came close to the rusty paintwork of a plumber's van, and the sharp, metal edge of the tray of a builder's lorry. When it seemed that the path was clear, and Helmut was signalling a success, Mrs Temple shot the car back impetuously, hitting a low wall, and breaking bricks off the top.

David watched Mrs Temple alight, slam the driver's door, and start remonstrating with Helmut. She gesticulated, pointing to a dent and a scratch on the otherwise pristine paintwork at the rear of the vehicle. Helmut's shoulders seemed to bend under the weight of Mrs Temple's unheard words.

The car was like a beached whale, until Keith came into the lobby. He saw the problem, went outside, had a word with them, and slid into the driver's seat. After a few short manoeuvres, he backed the car away effortlessly, and returned in moments with the keys. In the meantime, Helmut had an opportunity to exercise his charm on Mrs Temple.

She was, nevertheless, seething with annoyance when she was let in the door. Helmut took her into his office, and it was some minutes before David was summoned.

Mrs Temple was sitting on a low chair, her long legs prominently outlined in her tight jeans. All the chairs were some inches lower than Helmut's. The room was small. Helmut was almost hidden by a fountain of flowers on the desk in front of him. He peeped over the top, his good-natured smile like a rising sun. David stood by the door, until Helmut waved him to a seat.

Mrs Temple absorbed David in one unwavering stare of her blue eyes. "This is the man, definitely," she said.

"David Thurgood, Mrs Temple," Helmut said, formally.

"Enticing my dog away."

"Perhaps not enticement. I think the dog is still attached to its previous owner," Helmut said, very gently.

"I've been told that this man called the dog in the park, and it came to him, and the dog-walker couldn't get it back."

"I'm sure David wouldn't do that. David?"

"And a man had to intervene and help her!" Mrs Temple added.

"I … only…"

David didn't want to lie, but there wasn't enough space, and time, in the small room to explain that he had unintentionally frightened the dog-walker, and a stranger had got the wrong idea about what he was doing. The very explanation could give rise to other contentious points.

"He hasn't got anything to say!" Mrs Temple jeered.

"David can't always express himself."

"He doesn't need to. It *was* him. The dog-walker

described him. And as you know Mr ..." she nodded toward Helmut, who said, "Helmut."

"As you know, Mr Helmut, I had already met this man, when he tried a phoney trick about dog-walking on my doorstep."

"We haff a little identity confusion here."

"No, we don't," the woman said, rising up to stand in her full spidery height, looking down on Helmut, behind his bowl of flowers.

"If not identity confusion, then I think a little confusion about David's motives," Helmut pressed in a low voice.

"I don't give a monkey's about Thurgood's motives, Mr Helmut! *He's stolen my dog and I want it back!*"

"Never stolen, Mrs Temple. Never! David?"

David shook his head, no. "Poppy runs away."

"Don't give me that likely story! After what you've done, assaulting my dog-walker!"

Helmut rose up from behind the flowers, his palms held up to catch inspiration from above. "What can vee do?"

"It's up to you to safeguard the public from people like him," Mrs Temple said, with a jerk of her head toward David, "and not let him wander about the town stealing people's property. And let me tell you, I'm going to report this to the police, *and* I intend to complain to the medical authorities, or whoever it is that licences this ... *place,* about your failure to control the inmates!"

Mrs Temple burst out of the office. Helmut's face crumpled with alarm.

"David, it's war!"

David walked up the corridor from Helmut's office a few seconds later, and found that Mrs Temple's triumphal exit had come to a halt inside the locked front doors. Mrs Temple stood, ramrod straight, and fuming. Kay, the receptionist, was engrossed with two or three residents who were bent over her desk. Kay looked after residents' pocket money, expenses for outings, and answered the phone, as well as supervising the comings and goings through the doors. Delays were normal.

"Will you please let me out of this place!" Mrs Temple said in a raised voice, but the noise level was high, and nobody had noticed her.

When she saw David ambling along, she said shrilly, "*Will you let me out?*" in an accusatory tone, as though he was detaining her.

"Sorry, I don't know the numbers," David said pleasantly, although he didn't feel very well disposed towards her. "But I'll get somebody."

As David turned away, Barney Colas, fully dressed today in shirt and trousers, saw the problem. "Allow me, madam," he said, reaching confidently for the keypad, and tapping in a sequence of numbers. When the door did not open, because Barney did not know the combination, he pronounced it defective.

"I'm afraid we'll have to call our locksmith, lady, and in the meantime, you'll have to stay with us," Barney said graciously. "Our prisoner. Can I offer you lunch in our dining room?"

"This is unbelievable!" Mrs Temple said, her voice rising to a shriek.

Keith, who was almost omnipresent when there was trouble, was amongst them now. He brushed Barney aside, and opened the door. Mrs Temple did not acknowledge him, as she stamped out on to the porch.

14

David had a sense of intimacy with Caroline Higgins, if not closeness in spirit. He liked her. She was an agent of the world of rationality. He knew her mission was to make him fit into that world, to lever him into a box, the dimensions of which she, and his father, had set. He didn't resist. Indeed, he would have fitted in if he could. Caroline wanted to welcome his return to an order which was organised, predictable and just. She wanted everything to be 'just so', and believed it ought to be so, and generally was so. People like David – or Cathy – who were outside this order, were viewed as irretrievable, unnatural or mad.

The reservation David had was that Caroline didn't seem to appreciate the evidence of her eyes – that everything, every moment, was uncertain and likely to be chaotic. Nothing fitted into boxes, without the likelihood of jumping out. A red, chrome, steel monster, waited around the corner for everybody. What little David knew of his own past had taught him that.

Perhaps life at Denby Hall was more disordered and uncertain than it was outside. But it was a kind of chaos Helmut knew how to manage. When Mark Demeter, thumbs in his wide red braces, held a political meeting in the hallway, the staff took no action except to cheer him on. When Barney Colas writhed on the floor in a temper tantrum, blocking the dining room door, Keith would reason with him coolly. When Crispin Taggart put his boot through a pane of glass in the front door, he was led away without a rebuke, and the staff painstakingly fitted a temporary piece of cardboard over the hole, as though such events were routine. The raw steak that John Murdoch placed on Helmut's desk, without a plate underneath it, as a protest against the private cooking arrangements, initiated a serious inquiry.

Hilda Trennor was part of the disorder. She was the art teacher. Hilda was small, serious and very thin, with lines around her mouth, and hazel eyes in deep sockets. She was in her late thirties. She approached Cathy, Desmond, and David one day when they were in the sitting room, having afternoon tea.

"I wanted to show you some of Cathy's work," she said to Desmond, sidling up to him in her girlish way.

"Oh, very interesting," Desmond said, standing up, and taking the portfolio that Hilda handed to him.

Hilda moved to Desmond's side, and began to turn the sheets of paper in his arms slowly. Cathy, her attention on the pair, started to make a noise. "Arrrrgh!" Her arm was raised and swung around menacingly, her hand closed in a fist.

David knew that Cathy was protesting at Hilda's presence. Cathy didn't like Hilda. She said Hilda was 'bossy'. She had voluntarily withdrawn from the art class, months before her attendance at all classes had been officially stopped.

"Do you want a ciggy, dear?" Desmond asked Cathy.

He tended to treat every cry as a request for a cigarette. Cathy shook her head negatively, and made her distinctive, throaty noise, "Arrrgh! Arrrgh!"

She seemed to be particularly angry that her paintings were being shown to Desmond. And her earlier comments to David had shown that she thought Hilda paid too much attention to Desmond. David was uncertain what to do. He could hardly reveal this in front of Hilda, besides, he thought Cathy's jealousy was unjustified.

"I don't think Cathy wants a cigarette," David said, faintly.

"Oh, I think she does," Desmond said, beckoning a care assistant. "What else could be troubling her?"

"She's..." David began. He was going to say that Cathy hated the portfolio of paintings, but then he would have to add that Cathy hated them because Hilda had stood over her and practically painted them for her. This was another reason he couldn't explain in front of Hilda.

Desmond ignored David, and bulldozed on. "Ciggy time," he said, dismissing Cathy.

Cathy was wheeled away, protesting with all the volume of her lungs, and Desmond gave his attention to the portfolio.

He looked down at Hilda warmly, "Cathy used to be very good with pencil and paint, you know. Quite a skilled watercolourist. All the accomplishments of a well brought up young woman."

He paused to concentrate on each of the paintings, one by one.

"She's still very good, Mr Marsden," Hilda said. "Look at these."

What Desmond and David saw, was a series of bright, rainbow-like designs with a very blurred, and somewhat romantic feminine figure, dressed in flowing robes. The acrylic colour had been applied to wet paper. The paintings were all consistently, the same simplistic style. They showed a firmness of intention. There was nothing arbitrary or unconsidered about them.

Desmond had an amused and questioning look. "Are you sure these are Cathy's?"

"Of course, why else would I show you? I have a written record of everything she did," Hilda insisted.

"I heard she quit the class, before she was dropped from the house timetable."

"That was very unfortunate, Mr Marsden. These paintings were done beforehand. I hope she'll come back now for special one-to-one lessons."

"Why do you keep a record, Hilda?"

"It's for Cathy's file. It shows what she can do."

"I'm not clear about this. When Cathy was at home, and attended the day centre, she used to paint. A few shaky lines, and blotches. A mess. I saw all her stuff. She'd always bring it home. She'd lost her capability to do anything realistic at all, let alone a considered abstract."

"Mr Marsden, I've been teaching her," Hilda said, proudly.

"With all the teaching in the world, I don't see how she could have done these," Desmond said, flatly. "I mean, they're just not her. She never in her life did this sort of quasi-religious, mystical thing."

Hilda looked up at Desmond as though his misunderstanding was childish. "She's very talented. We used to read Ted Hughes together."

"The poet? Seriously? I can't believe it."

"Yes, we had nice times."

"Nice times reading Ted Hughes together?"

"Oh yes, we were really close."

"Tell me, why did Cathy quit the class?"

Hilda blushed. "I thought you knew. Cathy thought we, you and I, were having an affair."

Desmond showed distaste. "But I've only talked to you a couple, or three or four times!"

Hilda raised her eyebrows enigmatically.

Desmond glanced at David, and smoothed his black locks in perplexity. "God alive! These paintings, Ted Hughes' poetry, and an affair to boot. *Were* we having an affair, tell me that, Hilda?"

Desmond thrust his face toward Hilda's, and spoke in a melodramatic, theatrical voice.

"You know the answer to that, Mr Marsden," Hilda said shyly, gathering the paintings together in the portfolio.

When she had gone, Desmond let out a loud moan. "David, am I going mad? Am I mad already? Cathy never painted those paintings. Never. And she wouldn't know Ted Hughes from Dan Brown."

David grinned, "The paintings show what a good teacher Hilda is."

Desmond said he knew who Ted Hughes was, but he'd never read a line of his work. He couldn't imagine how Cathy, who had hardly touched a printed page in twenty years, would have had the faintest interest in the poet.

"I don't know about the poetry, but for the paintings, maybe Hilda held Cathy's hand, with the paint brush in it," David suggested, remembering the will signing.

15

In all the time David knew Cathy, her brother visited only once, and her sister, never. Simon Hurst arranged a visit with Helmut close to Cathy's fifty-second birthday. Simon arrived by taxi, on a sunny Monday afternoon in July, bearing a bulging bunch of lillies. He also had a box of chocolates, and a gift-wrapped present in his arms. He swung clumsily about in the lobby, shaking hands with Helmut. The pollen from the lillies stained Helmut's fawn jacket.

Simon was small and slender, with a tan and a well-developed chest. Youthfully dressed for a man in his late fifties, he wore scrubbed blue jeans, brown cowboy boots with slightly raised heels, and an open-necked shirt. Helmut had told David that Simon was a chemist in Norwich, with his own business. David could see no family resemblance to Cathy.

Helmut introduced David as a resident, who was a friend of Cathy, and could assist with the wheelchair, and information about the Hall. Simon had a look of slight concern at this.

"It's all right. David's nearly recovered, and he'll be leaving us soon," Helmut said reassuringly, and then Simon seemed grateful for the promised help.

"How is my sister?"

"She's a very complex case," Helmut said.

"We thought we should see her," Simon said

His expression implied that this was very difficult. Cathy

was inaccessible, but despite the difficulties, an inspection had to take place.

"We?" Helmut asked, looking out towards the porch.

"The family, in my position as eldest," Simon said, paternally.

"Cathy's general health is good, but there's no remission," Helmut said, mechanically.

"Quite. The family wanted to remember her birthday."

"Good." Helmut gave an embracing smile.

"We can't get down here easily, you know."

"From Norfolk? It's a long way."

"Very, but her birthday ..." Simon drew himself up positively.

His pectorals flexed, and tightened his shirt.

"Certainly, her birthday...." Helmut nodded the conversation along.

"Does she have many visitors?" Simon asked, with deliberate casualness.

"Her husband, quite regularly," Helmut, an expert in non-disclosure, said.

"Yes, of course. Her husband ... but we brothers and sisters, you know..."

"Don't feel the same?"

"I wouldn't say that ... It's very hard for us, and such a long way to come."

"What iss hard Mr Hurst?"

"Well, the ..." Simon said, raising his arms uncertainly. "Having this in the family..."

"It's difficult to accept," Helmut conceded.

"Will she know it's her birthday?" Simon asked, suggesting that he assumed Cathy wouldn't know.

"Mr Hurst, it's your visit that's important to Cathy," Helmut said. "Even if there's no occasion."

"But if she doesn't know..."

"She knows," David said firmly, and they both looked at him, surprised.

David wheeled Cathy into the sitting room to meet her brother. She spent only a moment of her attention on him. He sprang up from the couch, kissed her brow, and fondled her arm. David saw that Simon was affected by what he saw. The once slenderly mobile, amusing and clever sister was now a forbidding bust in a chair.

"It's wonderful to see you, Cathy, and I've brought this for your birthday."

Simon turned to the couch behind him. He picked up the gift wrapped parcel with a flourish. He placed it on the soft tray, which was fitted over the arms of the wheelchair, across Cathy's lap. Cathy looked from the parcel to Simon, and then out of the window. The pigeons were flying.

"Please, open it," Simon said.

Beverly was standing near, watching. "I don't think she can, Mr Hurst. Would you like to do it?"

"It's ladies' stuff, you know…"

Beverly accepted the task. She ploughed through layers of bright wrappers, and plastic covers, while Cathy watched the pigeons. What was eventually revealed was a purple cashmere sweater, a pair of black silk slacks, and a pyjama set, with blue and pink teddy bears embroidered on the chest.

"Aren't they stylish?" Beverly said, holding them up in front of Cathy. "And super quality."

Cathy had no eyes for them. Her bleary, inexpressive stare swept round the room, and then to the movement of the pigeons outside the window.

Simon looked pleased. "We know how fond Cathy is of teddy bears."

Beverly began to examine each piece more carefully. "Oh, dear. They're all size twelve," she pronounced.

"That's right," Simon said, smoothing his hand over the slacks proprietorially. "My sister told me. She actually purchased them."

"Oh, dear," Beverly said, again.

"What's wrong?"

"Cathy's size eighteen now."

"Size eighteen?" Simon said, his voice going up a note. "What's happened to her?"

Simon glared at Cathy. Seated in her wheelchair in a loose sweater, with the tray across her knees, and her thin, rather long neck, Cathy showed no easily discernible increase in weight.

"She has a special high calorie pulp diet, Mr Hurst, and she's put on the weight in the two years she's been here."

Simon huffed, "You should be controlling her weight!"

"We are, Mr Hurst. She's right for her condition."

"We should have been told."

"I don't think we have your address."

"Marsden should have told us. He's always wanting to rub our noses in Cathy's problems in his dreadful emails."

"Cathy's weight isn't a problem," Beverly said.

"What are we going to do with them?" David asked, holding up the pyjamas.

"One thing's sure, you'll not get Cathy into any of those garments," Beverly said.

"You could give them to Eva," David said, mentioning a small, and not very well off resident.

"Wait on, David," Beverly said, "that sweater cost a bomb. Mr Hurst might want to take it back, and change the sizes, or buy something else."

David watched Simon wriggle between uninviting alternatives – giving away valuable presents, or taking them back to his sister, to be changed, and then returned to Cathy.

Cathy seemed aware that, in some way, her brother's visit

had been spoiled. She watched him distantly, with dead eyes. He snatched the clothes, and bundled them into one of the discarded wrappers.

"I'll have to think about it. What do you expect me to do? I come to the end of the earth, to see my sister, and now... *How are we to know?*"

"We?" David asked.

"The family!" Simon spat.

To David, Caroline was like a doll, made in a factory; slender, blond, with a thousand lookalikes, polished and near-perfect. Her oval fingernails shone, and her white hands were moulded in plastic. He could find her image in every Sunday newspaper and magazine. Often he thought he saw her walking on Brighton High Street, but when he looked again it wasn't her.

David talked with Caroline at first in a small room at the front of Denby Hall, looking out towards the drive and the road. He liked this room, because he could watch what was happening outside. One of the tenants of the apartments across the road had a wooden eagle on his balcony, which was meant to scare the pigeons away. Cars and buses rumbled past. Teachers, nurses, and carers whom David knew, were walking up the drive, or leaving the Hall. He could see people moving according to the timetable of Denby Hall; doctors, plumbers, electricians, refuse collectors, and therapists. It was reassuring to verify this while Caroline asked her questions. When she realised David's interest was focused outside the window, Caroline said nothing, but had the room moved to the back of the Hall for the next session.

David then looked out at a bank overgrown with creeper. There was a small lawn on top, which he could barely see because the room was below ground level.

Seeing that he was uncomfortable, Caroline said, "I thought we could avoid distractions better here."

"I don't think it's really a distraction to look out of the window. Although you and I talk about every s-subject, in a way we only talk about one s-subject – the gap between *in here,* and *out there.* Dwelling on what's out there is quite a good background for our efforts."

Caroline rarely showed any reaction except relaxed acceptance, but David thought she looked embarrassed.

"Oh, I want our talks to be as natural and easy as possible. Having the blind down in the front room would be …"

"Unnatural," he said. "But isn't it… unnatural to be sitting here staring at the creeper?"

Caroline didn't comment. She moved them back to the front room for their future sessions, without drawing the blind. David could watch the traffic of the day revolving around Denby Hall. He believed that what Caroline would really have liked was a cork-lined consulting room, without windows.

16

David had made a shelter behind the garages, with a couple of used apple boxes, and Poppy seemed prepared to brave the cold of the Denby Hall garden at night. David had been out walking with Cathy and Poppy in the morning, and they were returning. They had just reached the point where the cliff path joins the drive to Denby Hall, when a gaudy police car came past them and stopped near the entrance. Two bulky officers extracted themselves from inside the vehicle. They placed their flat hats on, levelled them, and turned towards Cathy and David. They had crackling radios, and other gadgets strung across their chests.

"Excuse me, Sir. I'm Officer Ryan, and this is Officer Bateman. Is that your dog?"

"No … it's Cathy Marsden's." David answered promptly, and without any fear of the police. Cathy had, to his mind, a claim to the dog. Getting into a temper like Mrs Temple, and calling the police, was what people did 'out there,' and David felt remote from it.

Cathy watched the two men, but gave no sign.

Helmut had seen the arrival of the police from his office, and soon came out of the front door, and approached them. David knew that Helmut had been worried that Mrs Temple would carry out her threat. In one moment, he had declared that she was a vicious woman who wanted blood; and in the next moment, he had said that she was momentarily a little overwrought. He said she would see how unreasonable she was. Helmut summoned a show of confidence to put the officers at ease, his hand in the pocket of his tan trousers and his breast-pocket handkerchief fluttering in the breeze.

"Can I help?" he asked, amiably.

The two officers turned to this more authoritative figure.

"Yes, Sir. We're investigating the theft of a dog, a golden Labrador, very much like the one this gentleman is leading," Ryan said.

Ryan reached for Poppy's collar, and she jerked away, growling.

"I'd like to see that collar, Sir."

"I can tell you what the tag says, officer. It says 'Temple, Eccleston Street'," Helmut said.

"I see, so the dog doesn't belong to Marsden, as this gentleman said. It belongs to Temple. And you, Sir, know that. What's your name, may I ask, Sir?"

"I am the proprietor of Denby Hall, Helmut Schniewind. The dog keeps running away from its owner, and coming here. We can't help it."

"But you are helping it, Sir. It seems this gentleman here is restraining the animal with a leash, and he says the owner is Marsden, but the collar says Temple."

"You see…" Helmut's explanation dwindled inconclusively, and his face puckered more deeply into lines of tension.

"What connection is this gentleman to you, Sir?" Ryan asked, indicating David.

"He's one of the residents."

"So he lives under your management," Ryan said.

"I wouldn't call it that…"

"And he has the dog, which he says belongs to Marsden," Ryan said, compiling his case.

"Poppy doesn't understand," David said, interrupting the line of enquiry.

"If you don't mind me saying so, Sir," Ryan said, turning to David, "It's you who don't understand."

"He's a sick boy," Helmut said.

"Sick or not, it's not a matter of what the dog wants. It's the property of Mrs Temple, and she says that it has been stolen by a David Thurgood, whose description very much fits this gentleman."

"David means, officer, that the dog is still attached to its previous owner, Catherine Marsden, this lady here."

The two officers looked down at Cathy, as though they were seeing her for the first time. Motionless, she stared back at them. They were slightly baffled by the remote woman in the wheelchair. They appeared to understand that they could not address her, and returned their attention to Helmut and David.

"It's not about who the dog is attached to, Sir. It's not about the emotional life of the dog. The dog is property. Valuable property. Specifically, the property of Mrs Anita Temple," Ryan said.

"Yes, I understand, quite," Helmut said.

David started at the name 'Anita.' Cathy remained calm, and may not have heard. Had David heard correctly?

"What is the owner's name, did you say?" David asked.

Ryan repeated the full name and address. David had thought that Mrs Temple was an ordinary person in the street who had purchased a dog. Anita was a relatively uncommon name. It was too much of a coincidence that there could be two Anitas, one a stranger who bought the dog, and the other, Desmond's woman friend. Perhaps he should have thought of the possibility that Mrs Temple could be Anita, but what had fooled him was that Mrs Temple lived altogether separately from Desmond, in her own house.

"Shall we take custody of the animal?" Bateman asked Ryan.

"Recovery of the complainant's property, yes."

When Bateman made a move to take Poppy from David, she pulled away, the leash trailing on the ground. Poppy retreated a step for every step of the advancing officer. Bateman shouted, "Gotcha!" and jumped on the trailing end of the leash to halt Poppy. She leaped away with such force, that she tore the leash from under the soles of the officer's stout, black shoes. Bateman staggered, and nearly lost his balance.

"Bloody hell!" he gasped. "Nasty brute!"

The five of them, the two police officers, Helmut, David, and Cathy, were left in a rough circle, each – except Cathy – wondering what to do, or what would happen next.

"We have an ongoing investigation here," Ryan began in a deeper voice, taking control. He flexed his jaw to frame a suitably grave announcement. "And … I strongly suggest you return the dog immediately! I may need to take Mr Thurgood into custody later, to help with our enquiries."

The threat hardly impinged on David. What concerned him was that if Mrs Temple was Anita, she must have known all along that Poppy had belonged to Cathy, and yet she had chosen to act in such a petty way. He couldn't understand it.

Ryan eyed Bateman. Poppy had disappeared. Ryan flipped his chin toward the police car. The two officers lumbered to the vehicle, and when Bateman, the driver, had steered clear of the other parked vehicles, he accelerated away in an angry surge of gravel.

17

David's reaction, when he had to accept that Mrs Temple was Anita, was to consider her the one person in the world, ahead of any other, who should have taken a sympathetic view about Poppy's loyalties. Mrs Temple knew everything, yet she had presented herself as an innocent householder, in distress about her pet.

He began to try to remember what Cathy had told him about Anita. In the early days at Denby Hall, Cathy had said so much about herself. David had listened, letting Cathy's past fill his own empty landscape.

How did Cathy find out about Anita? She said she had always thought there was somebody else. Her physical life with Desmond was sporadic, and drifted to an end quite soon after marriage. Cathy blamed her illness. She could never *be* very physical. She supposed there had to be an Anita, and feared that there would be.

She said she had identified Anita very early. She was a family friend, married to another man. Desmond had introduced the couple. Graham and Anita had been guests of the Marsdens, and vice versa. Occasionally, they had dinner together or went to a gallery. Cathy met Anita's sister too. They used to sing in the same choir at St George's in Camden. They would go out for coffee and a chat after choir practice. Cathy would hear from Anita's sister what Anita was doing in the early years of the marriage. Anita's sister didn't divulge anything, if she knew, but it was too much of a coincidence that Anita seemed to be regularly in the same place – a town, or perhaps at a party, or other social function – as Desmond was. And Cathy had watched Desmond and Anita when they were in the same room together. Once, when they were playing bowls at a party at the Marsden's house, and it was Anita's turn, Cathy saw Desmond, as captain of their pair, place his hand on Anita's bottom, and whisper some instructions in her ear. It was the exceptional, and unconscious intimacy, of those who are physically close. She had heard Anita call Desmond 'Dear' in an unguarded moment. In Anita's vocabulary, 'Dear' wasn't a common coin. It became obvious to Cathy, from many supposedly innocent words and gestures, that Desmond and Anita were trying to cover up the fact that they knew each other very well, and far beyond the friendliness of dinner-party conversation. Cathy said that she could 'feel' the bond between Desmond and Anita when she was in the same room. It was like a magnetic field which repelled her, and made her heart shrink.

"However, I decided to do nothing, because I thought Desmond would do nothing," Cathy said. "I hinted about it, but we never talked. Desmond had two sensitive fronts in this respect. One was his children by his first marriage. He had already put them through an acrimonious breakdown, and I believed he would hesitate before breaking two more marriages, his own second one, and Anita's. He knew he'd lose face with his children, who were then teenagers. Another sensitivity was his image at work. He was a senior executive, hoping for promotion, respectably married for the second time. In those days, a steady marriage was supposedly the sign of a steady man.

"I was right. Desmond did nothing, except continue to see Anita occasionally. Of course, we ceased to see the Temples as a foursome. In the practical way of providing material help, and comfort for me, Desmond has been a good husband. And he looked after me personally in all the years I was imprisoned at home by the disease. My hold on Desmond increased rather than diminished with the years.

"Certainly, none of this stopped him 'secretly' buzzing off to Lake Garda for a long weekend with Anita. But if I try to see it from Anita's point of view – she lost Desmond to me, except for brief encounters, over the twenty years. I took over Desmond's life. You have to understand what that means, David.

"Marriage was the bond that held us together because Desmond respected it. That was the cause of our staying together. But people stay together for all sorts of different reasons, married or not. It doesn't really matter that *marriage* was the bond; it might have been something else, say love, or money or just plain habit. The point is, we were a couple, and once you're in 'coupledom', for whatever reason, illogical and unsatisfactory consequences often follow."

Cathy talked to David about what couples do to each other in alarming terms. She thought the slang phrase 'my other half', referring to a spouse or partner was accurate. She said couples were really one person, each with half a brain. She drew a strange picture of a being with four legs, four arms, and four eyes. But the creature had one brain, halved, and kept in two separate compartments in telepathic communication; a weird insect, sometimes at war with itself.

"You can be talking to a man about the rose garden he intends to add to his home," she said, "and suddenly you realise you're talking to his wife as well, although she might be in another room, or another town. When you know a couple well, you can see that they have ceased to be Janet and John, and become 'Janjon'. The lives of couples are twisted together like the branches of wisteria. The twisting and turning is partly involuntary and unconscious. It's not the sum total of the rational thoughts of two brains. It's the tangled decision-making of two half-brains, which interact, and may not connect properly. If you asked Desmond what the impact of my life has been on his, I suspect he would concede that it's been wrought into grotesque shapes by our coupledom. And yet, he has endured it.

"Desmond's been conditioned by what he does, like all of us. He's an engineer. He deals with practicalities. Grey areas have little place in his thinking. There is no room for 'might work'. All his life has been governed – and he's still steered – by what he regards as precise and measured thought. The irony of his life is how irrational, and illogical, it has been. And the reason for that is coupledom, and the convoluted decision-making of two half-brains. Even though my half-brain has little power left in it now, it still emits a tiny signal, which can have its effect."

To David, this was an alarming vision. He felt that in getting close to somebody, you could be subsumed within this 'couple' insect, and without realising, become a part of it. David had no wish to be *that* close to anybody – another concern for Caroline Higgins, who was always poking around to discover if he had a close relationship with somebody. David's father was remote, and not the material for a couple in Cathy's sense. David supposed that he himself was closer to Cathy and Poppy, than any other living beings, but not in the way that Cathy had meant.

Cathy said that her coupledom with Desmond left only ruins for Anita. And over the years, the emphasis had changed. Now that Cathy was hospitalised, and would never leave such an environment, Desmond was free to live with Anita. But Anita could not easily desert her elderly husband. Anita was bound to him by a sense of obligation. She was bound too by years of deception, which it would pain her to reveal.

"And I'm still in the frame, David barring the way to the joint property, needing some of Desmond's time to look after my affairs, which he gives, dwindling away the money he'll get under my will. Yes, Anita must see only ruins. In the hot blood of her early relationship with Desmond, it could all have been very different."

David saw that Desmond and Anita, too, were a couple, a deformed being, occasionally coming to life in holiday cottages, and hotel bedrooms, inhabiting them feverishly for a few hours, and then relapsing into a coma of telephone calls and emails, dominated for years by Cathy's needs, squirming under them, and still tacitly threatened by them. And now checkmated by Mr Temple's needs.

It may have been thoughtless of Desmond, in giving Poppy away, not to anticipate the turbulence that might be caused. But after thinking it over carefully, David could at least begin to understand Anita Temple's frustration and spite, in failing to win Poppy's loyalty, and hence Anita's uncompromising attitude towards him.

18

David was sitting in the sun, on the porch seat at the front entrance one morning, when Mark Demeter came out of the door, and stood facing the drive, rubbing his hands. Mark appeared to be alone, and to have slipped out of the door while staff, health professionals, and tradesmen were coming and going. He sometimes did this. The rule was that every visitor, resident, and staff member, had to be let in or out by Kay, and had to sign the record book, both inward and outward. But frequently, the door was held open by one person, as a politeness to another, and the record book got overlooked.

Mark was not allowed to leave Denby Hall unaccompanied, and David wondered whether he should alert Kay. Mark was wearing his best suit this morning, a dark blue chalk stripe, with a pale blue office shirt, and a red floral tie. His hair had been wetted, and slicked down. Mark's manner was to look you in the eye, and unselfconsciously begin a conversation. He could have been an alert, fortyish businessman. That was his backgound, in banking, until he had a fall while rock-climbing in Wales.

While Mark was standing expectantly at the edge of the paving, a car drew up. Mark gave an economical gesture of recognition with his hand. The driver got out, and shook hands with him. Brief words were spoken. Mark pointed to a space further along the drive, where the car could be parked. The driver accomplished this and retrieved his jacket and a file of papers from the back seat of the car. His bald head and face were pallid, and a paunch bulged his shirt. Mark escorted him to the door, and pressed the buzzer.

It looked to David, at first sight, as though the meeting had been prearranged, but he knew that it could not have been. He overheard Mark promising the man a complete tour of the Hall. Kay opened the door.

"Mulvaney, registration unit," the man announced.

Kay stepped aside, and Mark followed Mulvaney through the doorway. David was curious, and followed too. He guessed that Mark had seen Kay's diary of appointments – open on her desk – and moved to intercept Mr Mulvaney.

When the book had been signed, Mark pointed to a small framed photograph of Rudolph Steiner on the wall, and declared that he was the Hall's guide and mentor. The inspector smiled wanly. Mark took his arm.

"Most of the cases we have here are trauma cases. Did you know that, Inspector?"

"I know what your registration covers," the inspector said, cautiously.

"Motor cars. Motorcycles. Smashes. Deadly."

"Certainly. Tragic."

"But cars are beautiful and sexy, eh?" Mark leered, putting his face close to the inspector's.

"A modern preoccupation," the inspector said, leaning away.

"What I mean is, we don't have nutters here. No paranoiacs, schizophrenics, that lot."

"No, of course," the inspector agreed warily.

"This isn't a looney bin, Inspector. You're not at risk here." Mark grinned darkly, "Nobody is going to cut your throat with a razor, or try to choke you."

"That's a comfort," the inspector said, looking hard at Mark to confirm the reassurance.

As they moved out of the lobby, Mark pushed open the first door in the corridor, the smoking room.

"Alas, we have to provide for these poor misguided souls," Mark said, gesturing toward the dim figures in the haze of tobacco smoke.

The room was dark, and ill-ventilated; it stank of stale tobacco. The walls, once painted blue, were now furred with a brown stain. A large bucket of sand occupied the centre of the floor, littered with buts. Two or three residents were sitting quietly, talking and puffing. Their faces looked haggard in the poor light. One was a young woman with gapped teeth and a dress which hung low on her bare shoulders, almost showing her breasts, as she drooped on her chair.

"Watcha doin' Mark. Goin' to make a speech, then?" she cackled.

Mark ignored her. "Absolutely revolting, isn't it, Inspector? But enjoyment of life. That's why we do it, Sir! People have their little weaknesses, their little comforts."

The inspector flinched, and made a note on his file.

"We're not censorious. No, Sir. This is a liberal establishment. Enjoy, enjoy, enjoy."

"Really?" the inspector, said drily.

"And this lady here, Cathy Marsden is the owner of the dog you mentioned, the renowned, much loved and exceedingly beautiful Poppy," Mark said, pointing out Cathy in the gloom. "I suggest you ask her about Poppy. Cathy, this gentleman is from the local authority."

The inspector stepped forward. "Ms Marsden, we have a complaint that you are keeping your dog here, with the support of the management."

"With our complete support," Mark asserted.

"That's true, is it?" the inspector asked, looking from the impassive Cathy to Mark, and writing something.

"Absolutely," Mark said, opening his jacket, and sticking his thumbs comfortably behind his red braces.

"It's no use talkin' to Cathy, Mister. She don't talk back, do you love?" the gap-toothed woman said.

"I think I can answer pretty well for Cathy, Inspector," Mark said.

David was in the doorway, still debating with himself what to do, when he saw Helmut coming down the corridor rapidly. Helmut must have heard from Kay that the inspector had arrived, and begun his inspection. Helmut's face seemed to have contracted, and become very small on the whole space of his skull.

"Vot is happening?"

He grated out the words, as he pushed past David into the smoking room. He swung toward the inspector.

"Sir, may I ask your business?"

The inspector was about to answer, and then, taking in the foppish, but creased, and worn-down Helmut, and hearing the accent, said to Mark, "One of your patients?"

"Indeed yes, a very sad case," Mark confirmed.

"I'm dealing with Mr Demeter, the manager," the inspector said agreeably to Helmut, not wanting to further upset an obviously disturbed person.

"Most certainly," Mark said, puffing out his chest.

"Please! I am Helmut Schniewind, the licensee."

"He's a fantasist, Inspector," Mark said with assurance, and a grin.

"Interesting," the inspector said, with the faintest note of uncertainty.

"We humour him," Mark said.

For a few seconds there was a state of doubt between the three. The inspector, shaking his head in confusion; Mark, good-naturedly pressing his case, and not falling back one inch in his assertions, and Helmut, fumbling to withdraw his identification card from the folds of his jacket.

Keith came in the door, and sized up the picture in moments. "Come on, Mark! You shouldn't be in here. It's bad for you. Out! And you too, David. Out!"

The inspector's eyes sparked, and he reared his stooped shoulders up. "What's going on here? This is a mad house!"

Keith took Mark by the arm, and ushered him out of the room, leaving Helmut to deploy his considerable ability to placate the inspector.

The next day, David caught up with Keith, and asked what had happened, and what Inspector Mulvaney had said. Keith's face twisted painfully.

"He was highly pissed off, of course. Nothing about the dog. That was all bullshit, so don't worry yourself about it. But he left poor old Helmut with a requisition list as long as your arm. Replacement of carpets, repainting and redecoration of five bedrooms, new window vents in the kitchen, new extractor fans for the smoking rooms, and a repaint. You name it, we have to replace it. Thousands of quids worth. The guy dropped a shed-load of do-do on us. Well done, Mark."

"And Mrs Temple," David added.

19

After the police visit, Helmut, Keith, and David walked Poppy to Eccleston Street to return her. Helmet had arranged the visit with Mrs Temple, and wanted to apologise. When they arrived, the Filipino maid opened the door, and sought to take the dog inside, as she had apparently been instructed to do, and close the door as soon as possible. Helmut resisted this.

"Could I see Mrs Temple, please," Helmut said, while David held Poppy's leash.

The maid went away leaving the door ajar. David could hear the high tones of Mrs Temple's voice down the hall, as the maid explained that Poppy had not yet actually been handed over. The maid returned after a few moments, saying that Mrs Temple wasn't available, and could she please have the dog.

"I'm very sorry, but I would like to speak to Mrs Temple first," Helmut said stubbornly.

The maid turned her mouth down at the corners, and her eyes up, showing crescents of white. Something frightening was about to happen. She went back to her mistress. David heard even higher feminine notes. After a pause, Mrs Temple swept down the hall and threw the door wide open.

"What is this deputation for?" she demanded.

Her voice was slightly cracked, and her cheeks red. The bold colours of her print dress seemed to emphasise her agitation.

"Mrs Temple, we have met at my office, Helmut … I do apologise…"

Anita Temple was only checked slightly by Helmut's suavity, and his genteel appearance.

"Excuse me, but Justina must be returned to me. *Now.*"

"Certainly, certainly, but may I ask whether you would be prepared to sell Justina, please?"

Keith and David were astounded, and pulled curious faces at each other. Mrs Temple was surprised. David thought that after the financial consequences of the inspection, which Mrs Temple had provoked, it was a heroic offer.

"No. You've put me through hell for *my* dog."

"I'm deeply sorry. But the dog keeps coming to the Hall because it used to belong to one of the residents."

"No. The dog has been enticed away by that man," she pointed to David.

"Please, Mrs Temple, let us end our mutual problems in the easiest way."

"The problems aren't of my making, and they can best be ended by you handing Justina over, and never coming here again."

"You won't consider selling Justina under any circumstances?" Helmut said regretfully.

Anita Temple was appreciating that Helmut's proposal had some merit. She pressed her lips together thoughtfully. "How much are you prepared to pay?"

"Would fifty pounds be… reasonable?"

She let out a spurt of derision. "Don't waste my time! This is a valuable animal, a *pedigree* golden Labrador."

"How much, then?" Keith asked.

"Five hundred pounds would be a modest sum. I'm sure I could get more than that for her."

"You're off your rocker, lady," Keith said, flatly.

"Keith, please. I'm sorry Mrs Temple, we don't have that much money," Helmut said.

Anita Temple's eyes shone. "Well, that's it then. Give me the dog, and don't let me see or hear of any of you again."

She took the lead from David, and pulled Poppy over the threshold. "That's my lovely Justina!"

As they walked back disconsolately to Denby Hall, Keith said to Helmut, "It was a neat move to offer to buy Poppy."

"Vell, it's a solution, but an expensive one," Helmut laughed.

"Mean old bitch!" Keith said.

David said, "I didn't realise Poppy cost such a lot of money."

"She's a fine creature. Perhaps I vos being insulting in mentioning fifty pounds," Helmut said.

David was the only one of them who knew who Anita Temple really was, and therefore the only one to understand her meanness. But he was still convinced of the simplicity and effectiveness of what he wanted to do.

"Cathy need only see Poppy for a little time," David said.

"Yeah, and wouldn't you think that could be fitted in for less than five hundred quid?" Keith said.

"Maybe it can," David said.

"Pie in the sky, David," Keith said. "That old cow will never budge."

But David thought that Anita Temple's strained handling of the meeting showed that she understood how badly she was behaving – and she might relent. In a way, this behaviour apart, he quite liked her, and couldn't help feeling sorry for anybody entrapped for years in the dysfunctional Desmond-Anita couple and, at the same time, trapped in the worn out Anita-Graham couple.

20

David's presence as a helper with Cathy had become routine on Desmond's visits. When restaurants and coffee shops had become impossible, and Cathy had no obvious appreciation of a garden or a view, the only activity left to them, apart from playing films and discs in her room, was a walk along the cliffs. They used to walk slowly with Cathy's wheelchair for about half a mile east, or half a mile west toward town, weather permitting. David pushed the wheelchair. Desmond walked slightly behind and to one side of him, his hands clasped behind his back, like a dignitary accompanying a head of state at a public engagement. In the later days, Cathy and David spent their time together in silence when they were alone. But when Desmond joined them, he seemed unable to bear the silence, and felt obliged to talk.

Often some small event at Denby Hall would lead Desmond to recount his experiences with Cathy. And he would occasionally speak of things which might be too embarrassing to admit to his peers. In talking to David, he was not strictly sharing a confidence. He was mainly addressing himself. He expected no reply, no criticism or argument, and he got none. Desmond wanted to lay out his position, and reassure himself that it was as solid as he believed it was. David understood this. How much Cathy in her wheelchair heard or understood, David did not know. She never gave any sign that she followed, or was affected by any of it.

One day, Desmond began, "You see, David, the trouble with madness is that it seldom comes to life fully formed, like a new born baby. At first, madness is a mere absence of brightness in the house in which you live, then a haunting shadow, then a soft and palpable darkness around your actions. Before you realise it, if you're lucky enough to have a flash of insight, your life is deformed. You're a participant in the madness of the mad person. If I had fully understood the affair of the McFisheries jacket, I'd probably never have married Cathy. But to me, in those days, it was trivial, an irritation, not a warning.

"Cathy's brain lost power over many years. Now, of course, it's very obvious. Her brain can't control her speech or movement. But twenty years ago it began to fade, almost imperceptibly. And the toll of those years of fuzzy deterioration, of lack of focus, of inability to concentrate, has been agonising in practical terms. It's brought misery to both of us. And I suppose you'd say the interesting point about the brain of an intelligent woman like Cathy, is that it retained sufficient intelligence, even as it was failing, to work out devious ways of concealing its condition."

Desmond told David about the McFisheries jacket, a very old and worn plaid garment with a dark brown check, purchased from a department store that had long since ceased business. Cathy bought and owned the jacket before they were married. She liked the jacket. It was warm, and suited her image on the housing estate where she worked. The cuffs were frayed. A sleeve had been torn and roughly stitched up. The lining showed through at the elbows, and there was a shiny patina on the lapels. She wore the jacket frequently when she was working.

As soon as Desmond saw the garment, he said it was disgusting, and suggested that Cathy should throw it away. He offered her the money to buy a new one. And the fact that this lone garment gained a particular name, 'McFisheries' showed that it became an object of critical attention between them.

One day, when Cathy was wearing the jacket, they went into a pub to have a beer. Desmond left her at the back of the crowd, and pushed through to the bar to buy their drinks. A man approached Cathy while she was on her own. He was probably homeless. He was dirty, unshaven, and dressed in filthy clothes. Cathy was used to dealing with such people, and she took no offence, nor made any remark to drive him away. When Desmond appeared with the drinks, glowering, the man winked in a friendly way, and scuttled off.

'What did *he* want?' Desmond demanded.

'He asked if he could buy me a drink,' Cathy said.

'What did you say?'

'I declined,' Cathy laughed.

'It isn't funny. That man was a bloody tramp, trying to pick you up!'

'Maybe he was.'

'Now do you understand what a slag you look!'

"Cathy didn't reply. But I think she understood for the first time, the impression she presented in the jacket. She put it into the rubbish bin that night without any contest. I didn't appreciate it at the time, but there was something more than eccentricity in Cathy's attachment to the jacket. Later on, after we were married, there were lots of strange events which I interpreted in Cathy's favour. I dignified them with a logical justification. I bestowed rationality on them, although, like the McFisheries jacket and the pink bathroom, they were irrational."

The instance of the pink bathroom particularly irritated Desmond. He talked about it in a self-critical way. He said he had been keen to increase their fortunes by advances in the housing market. He and Cathy had had three homes, each one requiring considerable renovation, and each one improving their financial position quite strongly. Cathy could not cope with the confusion of a house full of tradesmen, and eventually got Desmond to promise that he would only propose a new house, if it required no work, and was ready to be lived in. Desmond found yet another house and, he believed, it met his promise.

Desmond said in a sorrowful tone, "It was a lovely house in Wimbledon, David, and a wonderful investment, but Cathy wouldn't move. I pressed her.

'Because it has a pink bathroom,' she said

'It's got a white one, too,' he reminded her.

'I can't use a pink bathroom. The colour upsets me.'

'You don't need to use it. Use the white one.'

'I can't bear a pink bathroom in the house.'

'OK we'll get it painted.'

'Desmond, you promised.'

'What's in painting a bathroom? The work of a couple of hours.'

'You promised.'

'Painting a bathroom isn't repair or renovation.'

'What is it?'

'Freshening up.'

"But it was no good. Cathy wouldn't move. And, do you know, David, I *accepted* that? I did. I had no idea Cathy was unwell, other than a bit depressed. I actually declined what was a valuable financial opportunity for both of us, because of the pink bathroom. It doesn't make any sense, does it? You see how a sane person can be led along a crazy path?

"When I found out that Cathy was seriously ill, I realised that this wasn't so much about pink bathrooms, or worn out jackets, as an inability to face change, a desperate, almost subconscious clinging to the things she knew.

"I could only see it with hindsight, but after we married,

Cathy began very slowly to avoid being put into social positions where her deficiencies, like her bad memory and her inability to concentrate, would show. She withdrew gradually from her more insightful friends. She withdrew from the social role of hostess and wife, which would have benefited my company commitments.

"At one point, I remember getting an anguished letter from Cathy's best friend. We hadn't seen Valerie and her husband in years, as a result of Cathy's surreptitious withdrawal, but at the time of our marriage we had met regularly as a foursome. Cathy and Valerie had done their social work training together, and shared some university research work. In her letter, Valerie was complaining that Cathy hadn't been in touch with her, and she was asking me why. Cathy was retreating to avoid being found out, and Valerie was upset, because she felt that Cathy hadn't made enough effort to see her. Valerie stayed at home and got angry, instead of getting into her car, and arriving on our doorstep. And there were lots of cases where we lost friends for the same reason. Friendships work like a balance sheet, David. If you don't return the dinner a friend bought you, you're unlikely to be invited again. Cathy used this method to shield herself. We didn't give any invitations, so eventually we   didn't get any.

"The biggest con of all was Cathy's stance as a liberated woman. I know she was a genuine advocate of women's rights, but it also provided a cover for her. She said she wasn't going to be a 'company wife' and be towed around to social functions as an ornament to me. In this way, she avoided having to submit herself to the normal social criticism, and judgements, of friends and acquaintances. She participated less and less in dinner parties, and less and less in the dinners at the Grosvenor, the trips to Henley, Ascot, Goodwood, and Silverstone. At the time, inconvenient though it was to me, I had some admiration for her stance. Yes, I mean it, admiration!

"In the early years of our marriage, Cathy used to be a community worker on a run-down estate in east London. She had her own project, funded by the local authority. It was valuable work, but I didn't stop to ask myself why an intelligent woman with top academic qualifications, and matchless experience, would choose to hole up for so long in a housing estate. The answer, I believe, was that she was dealing with people who were uncritically grateful for her help, and couldn't see her deficiencies.

"Can you see how looney all this was, David? The shape of both our lives being subtly and unknowingly altered by the toxin of madness, or you could say, by Cathy's fruitless attempts to combat the toxin. We suffered the loss of friends, and an almost complete withdrawal from the society of other people.

"That was in the days before I knew anything was seriously wrong. I was merely the man with the poorly wife."

David had a vision of the Cathy-Desmond couple shrivelling slowly into a shell, increasingly blind to where it was going, moving away from the paths of other couples, into a desert.

On Desmond's first visit, after the day Poppy had been taken back to Mrs Temple, Helmut found Cathy, Desmond and David in the garden. He leaned over for a few words with Cathy, and then shook hands with Desmond.

"You know Mr Marsden, we have had trouble with the dog, Cathy's dog."

"It's not Cathy's dog, Helmut," Desmond said baldly, in a tone which suggested that this was a touchy subject.

"I'm sure we're talking about the same animal."

"I had heard about the trouble it's been causing. I suppose

it's inevitable. The dog was used to Cathy, but it'll just have to get used to a new owner. May take time, but it's an intelligent beast. It'll learn."

"But Cathy…" Helmut began.

"As far as Cathy's concerned, I know she was fond of the dog, but I can't think that it's meaningful to her now."

"I think she is still fond of the dog," Helmut said.

Desmond nodded wisely. "Look, Helmut, Cathy's focus on anything, man or beast, is no more than a few seconds. I know that. You know that. Don't tell me that she's *fond* of the dog. She isn't capable of being fond of anything. I'm not here because she's fond of me. I'm here because I have a duty to perform. Cathy's no more fond of the dog, or me, than she is of her tooth brush, or her dinner plate."

Helmut's face creased tolerantly. "I think you are very wrong there Mr Marsden."

"Helmut, I like you. You do a marvellous job with all these people. But you read a lot of things into their minds, which for practical purposes don't exist. Cathy's virtually a … well, I don't need to say it … I'm not being rude or insulting about Cathy, or about your efforts. I'm being practical and factual."

"Yes, Mr Marsden, *you* are practical and factual. But Cathy …"

"Helmut, there is only one reality. The reality of you and me, here and now. We are alive, intelligent beings. Cathy is, by any practical standards, little more than a pulse."

David could follow the conversation quite well. Cathy simply stared ahead.

Helmut maintained his easy manner. "Well, I won't trouble you with whether there is any other reality than that of the sane, and intelligent. Let us talk about the dog." *

"Yes, the other thing about the dog is that I simply couldn't look after it. An animal like that has to be walked every day, it has to go to the vet, it has to be bathed and groomed, and it needs special food. Oh, there's no end of running around after it. And expense. I gave it away. Glad to see it go to a good home. People I know who'll look after it. I'm not callous about animals."

"You gave Poppy to Mrs Temple?"

"Yes, she had to go for her own good."

"Can I ask whether Poppy is very valuable, because I was thinking of buying her."

"Oh, yes. Cathy never had any thought of money when she bought it. Got the dog as a pup."

"Mrs Temple wanted five hundred pounds, and we could never afford that. I was buying her for Cathy, and some of the other residents. They like Poppy."

"Five *hundred*?" Desmond's voice rasped on the 'hundred.'

"Yes. I offered fifty pounds. We can't have dogs here permanently as pets, of course, not in a home like Denby Hall. But I could take her personally, and having a dog around a little could be good for some of the residents."

"She asked for five hundred pounds? That much? I've been getting hell from Mrs Temple about the dog. It keeps on running away. I gave it to her, after all. And it's nothing but trouble!"

"The police came. David was accused."

"Yes, I know all that. Dreadful. I should have had the animal put down."

"I'm worried Poppy is going to run away again, and we'll have a whole lot more trouble," Helmut said.

Desmond's usually sincere expression had gone. His eyes reflected the light glassily, and his mouth crimped into a short line.

"I'll have a word with Mrs Temple," Desmond said curtly, and David wondered what he would do.

21

David met Paul Prosser in the first few days of his residency. Paul came to the door of his room, knocked, and asked if he could come in. David was lying on his bed, looking at the ceiling, and thinking of nothing very much.

Paul was the same short, fleshy build as David, but ten or fifteen years older, with fair hair. He had a red face, which looked swollen. The tip of his nose, his cheeks and his chin gleamed like tomatoes. His red-veined, shrewd blue eyes contrasted with the clownish appearance of his other features and he wore soft, dark, woollen clothes. He looked amusing, but David's instinct was to be careful.

He levered himelf up on his elbows, and gestured the visitor inside. Paul entered with assurance, took a chair, and reached for the clock on a side-table. He picked it up, examined it in a cursory way, and set it back on the table.

"I'm Paul. How are you liking it?" he asked.

"David … Too early to say."

"It's a fine place. What are you in for, David?"

"Amnesia. Car accident. You know."

"Scrambled brains. I know. Like a drink?"

"No. I'm not supposed to, anyway."

"Wise. Pity though. I can get you some any time."

"Thanks. No."

"Smoke?"

"No. Makes me sick. Like drink."

"Pity. I have a quality supply."

"What are you in for?" David asked.

"Me? I'm doing a life sentence. I'm the padre."

"Oh, sorry," David felt himself reddening. "I thought…"

"Don't be sorry. I'm just a visitor from the other madhouse."

"You're not wearing your dog-collar."

Paul explained that he was a Baptist minister, and Denby Hall was part of his pastoral round.

"What do you do here?" David asked, to break the silence that had fallen.

"Very little. Give people a few smokes. A drink. A bar of chocolate. Take them to the beach. Virtually nothing. The question might be, what can they do for me? Ha! Ha!"

"What about your congregation, they must need …"

"Baptisms, weddings and funerals. That's what they need, on demand. As and when."

"Nothing about God…"

"My God, no!"

Although he never partook of Paul's offerings, they spent time together talking with other residents, particularly the small coterie who liked to smoke or drink, and either couldn't afford to, or couldn't obtain supplies. Paul had met Cathy, and they liked each other. Cathy always wanted to smoke. In fine weather, they met in the garden. Cathy felt easy with Paul, because she said he lived in the universe of the disabled.

The sessions in the garden were treated by the staff as private meetings, in that they mostly kept away. David knew that Keith or Ian, whoever was in charge that day, watched them occasionally from one of the windows, presumably to make sure that everybody was safe. Once Maggie, David's key worker, came and had a couple of puffs, and went away.

During one of their meetings in the first year, Desmond called unexpectedly to see Cathy. Alice, a care assistant came into the garden to get Cathy, but Cathy was smoking, and refused to move. Alice should probably have taken Cathy's wheelchair and propelled her back to the Hall, but Alice was too timid. Eventually Desmond, tired of waiting, came into the garden, and found their little circle, squatting on a wall, and some old wooden boxes.

He stood before them, slim-waisted in his suit, wearing shiny, black, pointed shoes. "Hello. Having a party?"

He was greeted with sniggers, and snorts of suppressed laughter.

"Mr Marsden. Please join us. Partake of our good things," Paul said, holding out a pouch, and cigarette papers.

Paul pointed to a supply of paper cups, and a half-bottle of cognac sitting on the wall. Desmond sniffed strongly through his large nose.

"I don't understand," he said firmly, in the voice of one who did understand.

"Quite a tang, wouldn't you say?" Paul said.

"That's why you do it outside," Desmond said, striking a horrified expression.

"Oh yes, it's our little confidential gathering."

"Involving my wife…"

"Cathy loves it."

"It's what I like Desmond," Cathy said.

"It's against … it's not…" Desmond said, waving his arms about incoherently, while the party continued to smoke, and laugh, and sip the cognac.

"Are you responsible for this?" Desmond asked Paul.

Paul, slightly stoned, stood up, and bowed absurdly. "Paul Prosser."

"I know you. You're the pastor. I can't believe…"

"Bringing a little lightness, and joy to my flock," Paul slurred.

"Desmond, I like it," Cathy said.

"David, you ought to be ashamed of yourself," Desmond said, turning to him.

"It's a bit of fun," David replied.

Desmond had attained a high colour. "It's intolerable, and … and illegal! And I'll see Helmut about it immediately."

Desmond stalked back to the Hall. The group watched him go without concern, and carried on smoking, and drinking. But in a few moments, Keith appeared, and issued some cryptic commands.

"Better move your ass off the premises a-s-a-p, Paul. Take the weed, and butts. Give me the bottle, and paper cups, and I'll bin them. Everybody else, back inside. Go to your rooms, and take it easy for a while. Come on, get going!"

Keith's orders had an understanding edge, and seldom incited rebellion. The little party broke up docilely, and moved back to the Hall. About half an hour later, Desmond found David in his room, and told him that he wanted him to be present at a meeting with Helmut. Keith would be there.

Helmut sat in the high chair in his office overlooking them, grave-faced. Desmond gave a lurid version of what he had seen, drunks, and drug addicts, under the evil spell of a minister of the church, and turned to David. "Isn't that true, David?"

"It wasn't quite …that bad," David said.

"Keith, have you looked into this?" Helmut asked.

"When I went out into the grounds, at…" Keith replied, looking at his watch, and giving a precise time, which was about fifteen or twenty minutes *after* his first intervention, "… there was nobody there, and no signs of any party."

"What about Mrs Marsden. What does she say?" Helmut asked.

"She's not here," Desmond said. "I think she should be protected…"

"I think we ought to hear from her," Helmut insisted.

"I'm not sure she can give a reliable account," Desmond protested.

"Mr Marsden, the problem here is essentially about Cathy's care, and I do think we should hear from her."

Desmond reluctantly accepted that there was no escape from this reasoning. Cathy was found, and wheeled into the cramped office. Helmut explained what had been said.

"It's rubbish," Cathy said. "I never smoked any pot."

"None?" Helmut asked.

"Oh, Cathy!" Desmond interjected, crestfallen.

"Not a single, solitary joint," she asserted.

"Did anybody else?" Helmut asked.

"Never," Cathy said.

"Cathy, you know that's ..." Desmond said.

"Ah, there, you see, Mr Marsden?" Helmut said, hunching his shoulders in a gesture of impossibility.

"That's why I asked David to be here," Desmond snapped. "Cathy never tells the truth! David? Tell them."

"I don't know... I don't smoke myself."

"But you know what they were doing!" Desmond insisted.

"Nothing," Cathy said. "I told you."

Helmut balanced his hands like the scales of justice. "How can I tell what is true, and what is false?"

"You have a priest who supplies drugs to your inmates. It's incontrovertible!"

Helmut mused, almost to himself, "Paul iss a gentle man, well liked here, with a somewhat unconventional interpretation of his ministry perhaps..."

Helmut considered the problem, as though it was a great distance from the room, and very hazy.

"*Somewhat unconventional, perhaps!*" Desmond's voice ascended the scale.

Helmut returned his attention to the audience, clasped his hands, and embraced them all with the warmth of his quiescence. "Well, thank you for raising this matter, Mr Marsden. Cathy seems to be well, and happy. That is the important point. We shall certainly be vigilant about this kind of situation."

22

"In the seven or eight years before Cathy came here, David, our lives degenerated into a kind of hell. Losing the society of friends, becoming two castaways, is one thing, but this was another. Cathy used to smoke up to sixty cigarettes a day, and she would get up every half hour or so during the night. She often used to follow me around. I couldn't be in the bathroom for very long. She'd come and bang on the door, demanding a cigarette. I literally couldn't have a shower, or a shit in peace. She'd be completely hysterical if I didn't go out to her right away.

"I had retired to another bedroom long before this, because of Cathy's restlessness, but I slept with one eye open. Cathy couldn't be trusted not to set the kitchen on fire. She'd promised to go outside to smoke, but she didn't always keep the promise. She was already losing the ability to strike a match or hold a cigarette. I had to do that. I was the carer in a mad-house. I was imprisoned by duties I couldn't get out of.

"In the morning, I used to make Cathy's breakfast, to avoid the mess of food and broken dishes on the kitchen floor. I had to plead with her to stop trying to empty the dishwasher, because the casualty rate for crockery was so high. After breakfast, I would lead her to the bathroom, take off her dressing gown, put a shower cap on her head, and help her wash in the shower. This was a muddle of arms and legs, in which I usually got soaked. I dried her. I laid out her clean clothes for the day, some of them laundered by me.

"And there was no equity in Cathy's thoughts. She dismissed a stately West Indian woman I employed as a cleaner, because the woman saw my laundered shirts draped over a chair, and ironed them without being asked. Cathy didn't like the woman pleasing me. She was jealous to a degree that was laughable. By the way, Cathy has never ironed a single shirt – or, for that matter done any personal laundry for me – in our entire marriage! In the days when I thought she was sane, I rationalised this as the stance of an emancipated woman! What a delusion. In reality, it was the defence of a person who couldn't summon the concentration to undertake sustained tasks. It wasn't simply whether she could be of some small service to me. Cathy's inertia and inactivity extended over every area of personal and household care, for both of us. The vacuum cleaner, abandoned in the middle of the carpet, was symbolic of Cathy's condition, but I had no understanding of that, until long after she became incapable of using one.

"I had left the company with a healthy payoff, and started working as an independent consultant from home. I had the time. I didn't choose to leave the office because of Cathy, but because the money was too good to refuse. But my leaving, and Cathy's needs, dovetailed neatly. Funny, isn't it? After her shower in the morning, I'd dress her, a wrestling match with her uncoordinated movements, negotiating the belts and buttons and zips. I not only purchased and organised Cathy's wardrobe, I dressed her, from her panties up for years. I got quite used to the ladies' lingerie departments. I have to admit that Anita helped with some of the shopping. I started to dress Cathy when I caught her going out of the house one day with her brassiere on over her dress. You get to the end of certain passages of your life with a jolt. What else could I do but take over?

"I had to clean her shoes, brush her hair, tie it back and spray her with perfume. The last step, was to go through her handbag, to make sure it contained everything she would require when she went to the local authority day care centre for five hours. Tissues, cigarettes, lighter, pocket money, and the door key, which was attached to the bag by a chain. The carers at the centre, and on the bus, would supervise her use of these things. She couldn't use the door key herself, but felt panicky without it. Cathy was attached to her handbag in much the same way as the McFisheries jacket. It was a dirty, stained shoulder-bag about nine inches square, real leather that had seen its last days long before and had almost worn to holes at the corners. I bought her other bags, but she wouldn't part with this one. She clutched it as though it was part of her body.

"Cathy was collected from home by the council bus, and used to agonise that it would not come. Do you know, we had a screaming fit every day – yes, almost every day, as a result of her fear that the bus wouldn't come? The bus was variously late every morning, because it had to crawl around the houses, picking up other disabled people before it got to us. But oh, the blessed relief when the bus came, and took her away!

"Later in the day, she would be returned in the bus, and take her seat at home in front of the television, rising every few minutes to go outside for a cigarette. At this time, she could manage eating messily herself, but she never took her eyes from the coloured screen, while she ate the meal I had cooked for her. Then I had to go through the long procedure of getting her to bed, undressing, washing, cleaning teeth. Much worse than managing a child. At least a child cooperates with you some of the time. With Cathy, it was all a struggle.

"At this time, David, I couldn't go out of the house when

133

Cathy was inside, without taking a key and leaving a side window open. I remember twice, when she was inside, I had to get a locksmith to let me in. The first time, I had forgotten my key. I knocked, banged, shouted through the letter slot, but Cathy wouldn't open up. The second time, I had a key, but Cathy had put the safety chain on. I banged the door knocker like fury, and rang and rang the bell, but she wouldn't answer. The locksmith couldn't cut the safety chain, which was hardened steel, and had to break the door-frame. All this with Cathy inside! That's why I also had to leave a side window open, so I could climb in if I forgot my key. When these events happened, Cathy claimed that she was asleep, or never heard me knocking. I never got to the bottom of it. It might have been accidental, or it might have been some kind of gesture of protest against me.

"This routine ground on for years, until, as Cathy became more and more unmanageable, I began to engage, and build up, what became a regiment of carers, who came to the house at all hours, to wash Cathy, dress her, cook and clean the house. They were mostly sweet-natured West Indian ladies, very modest and dignified, but it was difficult to keep the same team together, because they came from an agency. It sounds easy, having a team of carers, but I had to be on hand to explain and manage these services. I had to fill in the gaps when a carer was late, or couldn't come. I had to be on guard during the long nights, when Cathy was wandering about the house, even though a carer stayed over to sleep.

"I used the word 'protest,' David, in relation to being locked out, but there was an undercurrent of protest from Cathy in all that I did. While I was prostrating myself in her service, Cathy absorbed everything that was done for her as her natural right, like a princess, and the focus was on my shortcomings – which I suppose, were many."

At Denby Hall, the Sunday morning visit to church was a regular event. It wasn't a strictly religious outing, but rather a jolly, in which about twenty residents and carers squeezed into two minibuses for the ride. Then they shuffled in the cold and damp pews of the Anglican Church on Ponsonby Road, where hymns were sung. The vicar was very pleased with this block booking in his tiny congregation, although the residents occasionally made disturbing noises. David usually attended. He couldn't work out whether there was a personal God looking after him, or a God who was simply *there*, but didn't give a damn about him, or no God at all. Like Mark Demeter's lectures, the church service was pleasing on the eye, and ear, and left no trace afterwards. Everybody seemed to like blaring out *Onward, Christian soldiers, marching as to war …*

Cathy had always been included in the contingent, until one morning, when a carer was placing her wheelchair on the hoist into the minibus, and she started to protest. She waved her arms, "Arrrrgh, arrrrgh!"

"She doesn't want to go," David said.

"Come on, Cathy, don't be cross, and hold everybody up," Rose said.

Rose did not attend church herself, but she was often on hand to help load the minibuses.

"It's very good for you, Cathy," Hilda Trennor, the art teacher, said.

Hilda attended church regularly, and might have had a hand in the odd painting on the walls of the Hall. Although all paintings were officially attributed to residents, past and present, a few paintings depicted, very hazily in the background, crosses, and girls with halos.

"Arrrrgh, arrrrgh!" Cathy said, blocking the tightening of the safety strap on the hoist.

"Why don't you want to go, Cathy?" Hilda asked.

"She told me, ages ago, she didn't like it," David said.

The process by which people were selected, or chose to go to church, was uncertain, but habit prevailed. Cathy continued to go because her carers knew of her fondness for music. They always readied her, and made sure she was on the minibus. Now, at last, she was making a protest.

"Oh, that's daft, David," Rose said. "You've always loved it, haven't you dear?"

"Did Cathy say why she didn't like it?" Hilda asked David.

David knew that Cathy's feeling about church resulted from her talks with Paul, the pastor, over the years. To the question, why was God so cruel and merciless to Cathy, Paul had candidly answered that there could not *be* a God who could be so cruel and merciless, and yet be Cathy's personal God. Paul admitted that his own faith in a personal God had dwindled away "like a packet of weed."

"Too many ... innocent children suffering, she said," David said.

Rose said, "That's got nothing to do with the church, David. I don't think you've got it right."

"Wars and earthquakes is what she said."

David was unable, with residents pressing around him, and talking, to explain the argument Cathy had developed.

"That's not the church's fault," Rose insisted.

"What's the problem?" Ian, who was the day shift manager that day, asked, seeing the blockage.

Rose, Hilda, and Ian looked at each other, trying to fathom why Cathy did not want to go to church.

"I should have thought it was a nice little trip for her," Rose said.

"I know she's keen on the choir and the singing, even if she can't sing herself," Ian said.

"And it's so good for her," Hilda echoed again.

David waited for the wisdom of Cathy's visit to church to come into question for Ian, and watched as he scratched his chin in perplexity.

"Too many wars did you say?"

"Batty," Rose said, "Cathy loves church."

The leading minibus was already loaded and locked and the engine had been started. A cloud of pungent exhaust smoke drifted back over them, as Ian raised a hand in resignation and looked at his watch.

"OK, take her back inside the Hall again, and get the bus moving."

23

"And then there were the occasions I *tried* to get away from the mad-house just for a few days, David. I say tried because you can't get away, wherever you go.

"Anita and I used to go away for occasional weekends, but I had one task I had to perform each day, a phone call to Cathy. She was at home, surrounded by carers. I dreaded these calls, because I never knew what to expect. Increasingly, they were fraught with tension, and sometimes, abuse. I felt, and Anita agreed, that the contact had to be made. How could I forgive myself if an accident happened, and I was out of touch, with everybody trying to find me? And so, whenever I was away from Franklin Street, I made my daily call faithfully, although there were times when I vowed I had made my last.

"The calls were too intimate to be made from a telephone box on the street – you know, traffic roaring past, brakes squealing, people shouting – and in those times I didn't have a mobile that worked from abroad. Usually, the calls were made from my hotel room. Inevitably, Anita wasn't far away, often in the bathroom.

"I can remember once, when Anita and I were skiing in the Dolomites, I put in a call to Franklin Street, and Mildred, who was in charge, picked up the phone.

'How is she, Mildred?'

'She's very upset, Mr Marsden. She's out of cigarettes.'

'But that's impossible. I left several packets.'

'She says she's run out.'

Before I could tell Mildred where the spare cigarettes were, Cathy grabbed the phone. I could hear her choking breath before she spoke.

'You left me without any cigarettes!' she howled.

'Don't be silly, I left at least six packets downstairs in the usual place.'

"Another hysterical yell, 'And there's no money here! I can't buy any!'

'You don't need to, Mildred will...'

"She yelled, '*Why aren't you here? Why aren't you looking after me?*'

"Afterwards, Anita came out of the bathroom of our hotel, into the bedroom, saying, 'I could hear her screaming from in there.'

"I finally sorted it out with Mildred's help. There were cartons of cigarettes in reserve, and Mildred found them. But can you imagine the effect of a telephone call like that, David? Were we being very wicked, dining in the mountains, with the moonlit peaks in view from our snug dining room, the gentle backgound music, the candles on the tables, the shining cutlery and crystal? Wicked or not, I can tell you, Cathy's screams rang in our ears for the whole evening.

"That wasn't an isolated case. I was in Oslo with Anita, and Cathy broke her glasses. That was a terribly hysterical session. I should never have called home. I always swore I wouldn't, but then I always did.

"After years of this, and the chaos at home, both Cathy and I were at the absolute end of our endurance. The scenes of rage and frustration, mine as well as hers, were beginning to degenerate into physical violence. She would think nothing of lashing out at me, and I gave her a shaking at times. It was the edge of the precipice, the edge of madness for me. For a few crazy seconds, at times, I felt like killing her. And I had the ever-present darkness in my heart that I was in a prison from which there was no escape."

As Desmond, David and Cathy walked the cliffs, Desmond talked in his modulated tones, sometimes waving his arms hopelessly. David couldn't help seeing, quite graphically, the four-eyed four-armed, four-legged creature that Cathy had described, the Cathy-Desmond couple, now with half its legs and arms failed, or failing, and half its brain rotten, writhing in an internecine war with itself.

Now that David had been able to consider everything that Cathy had told him, he felt sympathy for Anita Temple, but the problem was intractable. Poppy wanted to see Cathy, and at the same time, Poppy could also have a comfortable life at Eccleston Street. Therefore, if nothing was done, Poppy was likely to break bounds, and upset Anita. This would cause trouble at Denby Hall.

The new element that David had thought of in his proposition to Anita, was a promise by Helmut that Poppy would be returned to Anita scrupulously within agreed times. Anita might not believe David, but he was sure she would believe Helmut. David hadn't spoken to Helmut about the idea yet, but he was sure Helmut would agree. He hadn't worked out the precise way that Helmut's promise would be delivered to Anita, but that could wait until Anita accepted the idea in principle.

It was with this solution in mind, that David hobbled to Eccleston Street again, determined to brave Anita's wrath, and persist until he had made his point. He was not looking forward to the encounter. The prospect of the meeting had hung over him depressingly since he had conceived it a few days previously. David did not pause for further thought when he arrived at number 73, but hauled himself up the steps, and pressed the buzzer.

The door was opened this time, after a long pause, by an elderly man in a canary waistcoat and carpet slippers, with a wide, florid face. He moved slowly, and looked David up and down benevolently.

"I've come to see Mrs Temple."

"She's out at the moment. Back soon."

"About the dog."

"Oh, well. Come in," the man said, taking this as an assurance of serious business.

David followed the man into the reception room off the hall. It was decorated with voluminous drapes at the tall windows, Persian rugs on the polished floor, and a giant gilt antique mirror over the mantelpiece, with a slightly distorted reflection.

"Can I help in the meantime?" the man asked.

"I've come to ask Mrs Temple … to let Cathy see Poppy … you call her Justina … Helmut would promise to return her …" David dried up.

"Please sit down, Mr …"

"David …from Denby Hall," David said, sitting stiffly in an armchair with cabriole legs.

"David. Yes, Denby Hall. I know it. You live there?"

"Yes… While I recover from a car accident. I expect I'll be leaving soon…"

"Good for you. Now, what about Justina? I'm sorry, I didn't catch what you mean."

"Justina used to be Cathy's dog."

"Really? I know my wife bought her, against my suggestion to get a pup. She's a superb animal, of course."

"D–Desmond gave her to Mrs Temple."

"Gave her? I don't think so. Who's Desmond?"

"Desmond is Cathy's husband. Justina was Cathy's dog."

"Desmond… Cathy… Desmond and Cathy who?"

"Marsden... Cathy is sick. She's at Denby Hall. She'd like to see Justina."

"Marsden, Marsden. Unforgettable name. Important missionary to New Zealand in the early days, Samuel Marsden."

David could see that while Mr Temple was reflecting about history, at the same time his mind was racing to uncover memories.

"I do remember the name. Would that be the couple we used to know years ago?" he asked.

"I don't know."

"You say Mrs Marsden is now very ill, and Mr Marsden gave her dog to Mrs Temple?"

"Yes... and Cathy only needs to see Justina occasionally."

"Quite, but why should Mr Marsden give the dog away?"

"Because Poppy ... Justina was a nuisance."

"I mean, why give it to Mrs Temple?"

"I suppose, because she wanted it. Poppy's beautiful."

"I understand that Mrs Temple might want a beautiful dog, but why particularly give it to Mrs Temple? Why not give it to Mrs Snodgrass down the road?" Mr Temple enquired gently, looking past David, into the distance.

"Mr Marsden and Mrs Temple ... Desmond and Anita are friends, aren't they?" David asked.

"Desmond and Anita? Friends, are they?" Mr Temple asked, looking fiercely at David, but without raising his voice.

David could see Mr Temple's agitation rising. He couldn't quite understand what he should do to assuage it. "So I thought ... it would be only fair..." he began.

Mr Temple sat down on a Queen Anne chair, in as uncomfortable a posture as David's. He clasped his big white hands, and pushed them down between his knees, as though he had stomach ache. He stared at the rug.

After a half a minute of silence, the front door clicked.

142

Paper rustled in the hall. Anita Temple came into the room, carrying shopping bags.

"Oh, there you are, Graham. I've got …"

She saw David, and felt the grimness in the air.

"What are *you* doing here?" she said, hoarsely to David.

Mr Temple threw himself back in the chair, arms outstretched. "I've been hearing about your twenty year friendship with Desmond Marsden!"

Anita dropped her shopping bags, and pointed at David.

"This is ridiculous! Do you know who this person is? He's a madman from Denby Hall! He's the one who has been trying to entice Justina away. He's a liar, a menace, and a thief, and I've already reported him to the police. He should be locked up. You can't believe a word he says!"

Mr Temple spoke quietly, in an old fashioned, cultured tone, like a detective in a fifties film.

"I remember Desmond Marsden. Him and his wife. We knew them not long after we married. A few dinner parties, and they faded out over months. It's so long ago, I can't even remember why I disliked Marsden."

"You've been listening to irresponsible and stupid lies!"

"Anita, tell me. Did Marsden *give* you the dog you told me you had bought?"

Anita Temple screamed, a piercing noise, which prickled David's ears.

"Get out of here you lying little bastard! Get out, get out, get out!"

As David rose hesitantly to his feet, Anita grasped a vase on the mantelpiece, and threw it at him. He wasn't fast enough to dodge, and the vase hit his arm, and bounced off, smashing on a marble statuette which stood on a side-table. David swayed out of the room as fast as he could, and out of the front door, his back and legs red hot with the pain of the movement.

24

In his monologues to David, Desmond had started in an offhand way, frequently self-deprecating. But over the months, as he charted Cathy's decline, he became more serious. As he approached the end of his personal involvement with her as a carer, he was taut. His fingers trembled. He moved his head spasmodically. His voice was held down to a low, level tone.

Desmond and David were in the garden. David had sat on the wall and Desmond was standing near him, but not precisely addressing him. Cathy, huddled in a blanket, was in her wheelchair a yard or so away, and facing away. On this occasion, Desmond was dressed more casually, in grey slacks and a cashmere sweater. He wasn't in his usual stiff-backed pose, as though he was about to be photographed. He slumped.

"Cathy's admission to Denby Hall came after a cataclysmic night, which started in much the same way as hundreds of others. I heard her shout. I raised myself from my bed in the next room, and looked at the illuminated clock. It was three in the morning. I heard her kicking and muttering. I knew that she would get out of bed soon, so I rose, slipped on my dressing gown, and went into her room. Her hands and feet were twitching. She was wide awake, and holding herself in check.

'Do you want to go to the toilet?'

"She didn't answer, so I slid my hand into the sheets and

they were soaked. I complained loudly, and bitterly. Mildred, who slept in the small room beside Cathy's, was out of bed by this time.

'Don't worry, Mr Marsden, I'll change the bed.'

"I told Cathy to get up, and began to help her. Mildred found a dry nightdress, and with a struggle, Mildred and I removed the wet one. Cathy did not like Mildred – or any female carer – in the house at night, and this was reflected in bad temper, and lack of cooperation.

'A shower?' Mildred suggested.

'Damn the shower. Put on the dry nightdress and her dressing gown,' I said.

'Ciggy!' Cathy said.

"There was nothing unusual in this demand. It would be the first of the many cigarettes that Cathy would consume that day. And the demand could not be denied, unless we wanted to provoke an interminable, temperamental scene. I say interminable, because neither I, nor any carer I ever employed, had the will to hold out against her. Nobody had ever won this battle of wills, other than Cathy.

"I helped Cathy down the stairs, took her through the kitchen, and out to the rear patio. I lit a cigarette for her from the pack kept in the kitchen, and gave it to her. She sat on the patio seat, drawing lungfuls of smoke as though they were life-giving. It was chilly, and I put a coat around her shoulders.

"I went back upstairs, and helped Mildred finish getting the dry bed ready, and then went down to Cathy. She was standing, empty-handed, at the open kitchen door.

'Where's the cigarette butt?' I asked.

"There was no answer to this question. I had to begin the usual detective work. The patio lights showed that there was no butt out there, or in the ashtray. I spotted a fleck of ash on the kitchen tiles; it was a sign I recognised. A lighted cigarette had been thrown down on the tiles, and skidded under one of the kitchen appliances. I began to crawl along the floor on my hands and knees, looking into the small apertures under the dishwasher and the washing machine. I saw a glowing spot of light under the refrigerator. I had promised myself I'd keep a wire in the kitchen to fish cigarette butts out of difficult places; but I never did. A kebab skewer wasn't long enough, and I couldn't find a suitable instrument in the appliance drawer. The smell of burning was growing stronger. I went to the closet under the stairs, got a wire coathanger, wrenched it into a long hook, and eventually hooked out the smoking butt.

Cathy watched this performance impassively, before saying, 'Ciggy!'

'No bloody ciggy!' I replied. 'Get up to bed!'

"I went to the downstairs bathroom to urinate, with the packet of cigarettes I kept in the kitchen, in my dressing gown pocket. I knew that Cathy would take one if she could get hold of the packet, and try to light it. She liked to have two cigarettes in a row.

Cathy didn't go to bed. She followed me, and started banging on the toilet door, shouting 'Ciggy, ciggy, ciggy!'

"I decided, when I came out of the bathroom, that we would never get back to bed unless I gave in, so I lit her another cigarette, and left her outside. Upstairs, Mildred had finished Cathy's bedroom, and was waiting quietly for her to come up.

When I went down to the kitchen this time, I found the room full of smoke. Cathy had taken a few puffs – she rarely smoked all of a cigarette – and thrown the butt in the waste bin. The contents had caught fire, and perhaps in an attempt to right her mistake, Cathy had grappled with the bin, and upset it on the floor. Flaming pieces of paper, and cardboard from the bin were spread over the tiles. I filled a saucepan with water, and poured it over the floor, and into the bin, to put out the flames.

We went upstairs with the kitchen tiles swimming with water, and burn marks on the white painted walls. Cathy had singed her hands and the house reeked of burnt rubbish.

'You'll have to look after her, Mildred,' I said, 'and put some cream on her hands.'

"I wanted to scream. I went into my room and slammed and locked the door, while Mildred put Cathy to bed. I put a cushion over my head. I was determined that nothing would make me get up until it was morning.

"Faintly, perhaps ten or twenty minutes later, I heard Cathy get up again, and go downstairs. She would search the kitchen and find no cigarettes, because I still had them in the pocket of my dressing gown. Soon, I heard her clumping up the stairs, breathing stertorously, and grumbling under her breath. She tried to get into my room, and found it was locked. She banged on the door.

"I knew that a sequence had started which could not be ended without my personal intervention, but I was so angry, I clung to my pillow. The banging increased in power. Cathy was hitting the door with an article she had seized. One of the central panels in the door splintered. She was striking it with a paperweight from the upper hall table.

"I could hear Mildred remonstrating with her, trying to get her to go back to bed, but Cathy had a fixed desire for a cigarette, and would yield to nobody, especially not a mild mannered West Indian woman, whose presence she resented. Mildred, with the best intentions, attempted to restrain Cathy physically, and I could hear them struggling. I don't doubt that Mildred was gentle with her. Perhaps that was a mistake. Cathy was enraged. They were on the landing at the top of the stairs. I knew I had to concede to Cathy, and I sprang out of bed angrily. I unlocked and opened my door, in time to see Cathy, foaming, push Mildred down the stairs.

147

"Mildred fell ten or so carpeted steps, before being able to save herself. She was sore, but not seriously hurt. This event calmed Cathy. I told her to go to bed, and she did. I sent Mildred to her room, and covered Cathy up. For once, Cathy slept. I lay awake until dawn, my head throbbing, and then fell into a dead sleep for an hour.

"The routines of this particular morning were strange, because they took place in silence. Cathy smoked her usual cigarettes. She didn't resist Mildred or me, and didn't start shouting about the lateness of the bus.

"Mildred said to me, after Cathy had caught the bus, 'Mr Marsden, last night I phoned the emergency line.'

"I was too tired to bother to question her about the implications of this, but the manager of the day centre called me not long after Cathy arrived at the centre.

"'Mr Marsden, I've been talking to my office. We think it's necessary to take your wife into care before anything serious happens. I've seen her this morning. She's very bruised. Her arms. Her breasts. Her hands have open wounds. I've called a doctor to examine her. A social worker will see you this morning.'

"The woman was brusque. I felt I wanted to make an explanation, but my head was thick with fatigue. At least Cathy was out of my hands. I fell asleep on the couch in the living room.

"The social worker was at the door by eleven o'clock that morning, a dark-haired girl in a black jersey and skirt, with a worn haversack over her shoulder and white trainers on her feet. 'Jacky' as she introduced herself, came in looking alertly about the hall and sitting room, perhaps trying to assess the kind of people she was dealing with. Mildred brought her a cup of tea. Mildred's shift had expired, but she had stayed on for the meeting.

"Jacky pulled a thick notebook and a ballpoint pen out of

her bag, crossed her legs, and made herself comfortable, with the notebook on her knee.

'Now then,' she said with a formal smile, 'We are thinking that Mrs Marsden should go by ambulance from the day centre today, without returning here. If Mildred could pack her bag. Denby Hall is where Mrs Marsden has been on respite care twice, and we think that is the right place. Our finance department will be in touch with you about costs later.'

"The suddenness of it was both a shock, and a release. The words 'without returning here' were actually a blessed relief. They echoed in my head.

'The doctor has seen Mrs Marsden, and she has … had a bad time,' Jacky said.

'So have I,' I said.

'Quite so. At this point, violence from both parties is perfectly understandable, Mr Marsden. I'm not being critical, believe me.'

'But you are. I haven't been violent.'

Jacky nodded seriously. 'I understand what you say. You see it one way. Mrs Marsden would see it another way. That's natural.'

'For Christ's sake, I haven't touched my wife!'

'She is marked, Mr Marsden.'

'I didn't put the fucking marks on her!'

'Well, let's not argue about that, at this point. I'm not here to accuse you. I'm only here to inform you of our decision that Cathy Marsden is at risk, and to make the necessary arrangements. That decision is also based on our observations over the last six or so months.'

"It was true that there had been some physical violence between Cathy and me in recent times, but only those occasions that were so lunatic, that if I hadn't restrained her, worse would have happened. I understood that the local authority must have been monitoring her condition at the day centre. But I wasn't going to take the rap for last night. I turned to Mildred who was sitting straight-backed, as though the chair was alien to her.

'Ask Mildred,' I insisted.

'Mildred's explanation on the nightline was recorded.'

'Good. Surely she didn't suggest…'

'Oh, no. She's very loyal.'

'That's honesty, not loyalty!'

'Calm down, Mr Marsden,' Jacky said, putting aside her notebook and pencil, uncrossing her legs, and leaning forward, to hold me squarely with her eyes.

'Are you going to tell me frankly, Mr Marsden, that in all this suffering, you've never laid a finger on your wife?'

'No, yes, I mean…'

Jacky gave a little dimpled simper, and resumed her pose, notebook and pencil poised.

"David, no appeal from her judgment was possible. On top of this hell, I was a wife-beater as well!"

25

David retreated from Eccleston Street without much concern about Anita's abuse. He thought that she was a deeply frustrated person, and he could see himself as the immediate cause of some of her annoyance. At the same time, he had no doubts about the merit of what he was trying to do for Cathy. A bruise on his arm, a few pains in his legs, and a conflict which unfortunately upset Anita, was a negligible price to pay.

He was, however, extremely worried about his part in hurting Mr Temple. He had assumed that Mr Temple knew about the Desmond-Anita couple, just as Cathy did, and almost always had. After all, it was a friendship of many years. He lay on the bed in his room, and tried to work out what effect the knowledge of the existence of the Desmond-Anita couple would have on Mr Temple. Would he kick his wife out of the house? Murder Desmond? Commit suicide? David's picture of the Anita-Graham couple, in Cathy's terms, was that it was always a feeble and disorientated creature, and now had inside it a cancer that could be fatal. And he, David Thurgood, had unintentionally implanted that cancer, which would spread with fearful malignance.

Save that he would tell nobody in the meantime, he could not decide how to deal with his responsibility towards Mr Temple. It was a nagging worry. And he remained as determined as ever to find some way to enable Cathy to see Poppy regularly. His scheme of basing this on a solemn promise by Helmut had never yet been put, and he did not intend to abandon it. He still believed that, in the end, Anita would be gracious enough to agree.

Cathy had had her assessment which, as usual, took place in her absence. David wanted to know the result. He found Keith poring over books in one of the empty meeting rooms. When he butted in, Keith pushed his glasses up to rest on his hair, glad to be interrupted. It was unusual to see Keith sitting down.

"What are you doing?" David asked.

"Reading. Management and stuff."

"But you're already the manager."

"Yes, but I'd like the title, the money that goes with it, and not to have to do night shifts."

"Where does this new manager fit in?"

"Helmut's new regime. A full-time manager, as well as the two shift managers."

"Will you get it?"

"I've got hopes, David. I want to marry my girlfriend, and settle down."

"How was Cathy's assessment?"

"Not so good for us."

"You mean, Cathy's going to move?"

"I'd bet on it, but the Funders never let on. Maybe they have a view, but it has to be ticked off by a dozen big bosses up the admin pyramid first. Helmut'll probably get a call eventually, and then there will be contract negotiations…"

"What's that?"

"The Funders trying to wriggle out of their contract with us."

This didn't mean much to David, so he tried a different angle. "Why would Cathy be going?"

"Too expensive here."

David knew that Cathy required a lot of extra services. "But I thought it was about her needs."

"It is, and it isn't," Keith said, in the light way that he had of underlining what was meaningless, or paradoxical.

David thought that Cathy's needs were overwhelming, far greater than most, but not all other residents. She was really a patient rather than a resident.

Cathy moved a lot, but was immobile in any rational sense. She needed a bed that could be raised and lowered, to enable staff to access her. It also had to have soft sides to stop her bruising herself in the night, or falling out. She couldn't use a shower trolley like most disabled people, where a patient sits on a plastic seat, and is wheeled under the faucet. This would be dangerous, as Cathy, whose movements were often involuntary, might fall off the seat. Instead, she had to have a shower-tray, a padded table, with slightly raised edges upon which she could lie, while an attendant bent over her with a hose. The space required for a shower tray meant that the small ensuite shower-room in her bedroom was useless. A special tiled and drained cubicle, the size of a small bedroom, was necessary for Cathy's shower. Cathy was also doubly incontinent, and it took two, or even three people, to toilet her every few hours.

So many people were necessary for Cathy's safety. And the safety of the carers was also an issue. Cathy could not assist the movement process, and very frequently struggled against it, putting a variety of sudden and unexpected stresses and strains on her helpers. Once awake, Cathy had to be moved to meet the needs of daily living. Her 'transfers', as they were called, were accomplished by an electric hoist, manned by three people, the operator and a helper on each side of Cathy – bed to wheelchair, wheelchair to toilet, toilet to wheelchair, wheelchair to shower, shower to wheelchair, wheelchair to bed. Cathy was lifted up in a sling, like cargo being swung ashore to the wharf, from the deck of an ocean freighter. In addition, Cathy needed skilled hand-feeding, and dietetic supervision, because she was in danger of choking at any time. She had to have constant physiotherapy to keep her muscles in use, as a result of her bed and chair existence. She needed psychiatric observation to determine the appropriate treatment for her subterranean rages, psychotherapeutic help, and twenty-four hour availability of qualified nurses and doctors, in case she harmed herself in a screaming fit. Even occupational therapy was given by a serious young man, who also attended to David. He spent a lot of time trying to get Cathy to use her hands for a meaningful action, to no avail.

David thought of a whole nation, where the flame of life was held sacred, where the elderly and the sick, like Cathy, could only be kept alive by legions of health care professionals, equipped with complicated machinery. So many healthy people could become engrossed in keeping the unhealthy ones alive. The endeavour seemed to tip over into futility, as more and more people became old or sick, and required more and more helpers, to operate ever-developing and more complicated machinery.

And yet, wasn't the spark of life infinitely precious? His own life, a bit bent and broken, was a good life. Cathy's small light was precious. Just that morning, he had found a spider on his towel, in his bedroom. He had taken the towel down two flights of stairs, and outside, to let the spider escape in the bushes. He couldn't kill a spider. It seemed that the spider's life was valuable too. It was in relation to these confusing thoughts, that David considered Cathy's enormous needs.

"It is, and it isn't about her needs, David. At the Hall, we don't specialise in cases like Cathy. We can handle her, but we've had to take on extra staff, get more help from specialists, and buy a whole lot of new equipment. There are other places that can do Cathy more cheaply."

"But she still needs things like the hoist and that, wherever she goes."

"Yeah. The place I think she's going, they kinda operate in a different way. They're specialised. Really ga-ga cases. They get them up in a wheelchair in the morning, sedate them, and stick them in front of the television. They let them mess at their own pleasure, and clean them up once a day, in the shower, unless they've got bed sores."

"Is that all they do?"

"Pretty well. No rides in the grounds, because there aren't any grounds. No rides in the park, because there's no minibus for these patients. No music evenings. No wheelchair dancing. No calming room. No aromatherapy. No society. No trimmings. Probably on the sixth floor. Low maintenance. And relatively el cheapo."

David could see Cathy lying in a chair, with her head back, in a kind of broken-necked posture, her mouth open, staring at the ceiling of a solitary sixth floor room, a prison cell that was many times more chilling than her own personal prison cell inside her head.

"It's not that bad," Keith said, seeing David's repulsion. "High calorie pulp feeding, plenty of protective pills. These patients don't get ailments like people in the street you know, influenza, chills, coughs, lung infections. They could live to be a hundred, although their brains have turned to custard years before."

David remembered Cathy telling him about the sea cucumbers, living alimentary canals.

"Didn't Desmond try to keep her here?"

"No way. He's a hundred per cent in favour of the London home. He was very clear about that."

"But you told me his views wouldn't count that much."

"Ah, they do if they're the cheapest. That's when you hear officials beating the tub about being inclusive, and consulting the family."

"So it's all about money."

"David, you're so delightfully naïve. Of course it is!"

"But you told me it was also about Cathy's needs."

"I said, it is and it isn't. Don't you get it? The amazing coincidence between the two, cost and needs?"

"But there isn't a coincidence."

"Oh, yes there is. That's what the assessors, the panels, the husbands like Desmond, work on, making Cathy's needs fit the budget, refining them down to a beautiful 'coincidence'."

David decided to say nothing to Cathy about his conversation with Keith. Events were taking their expected course, and Cathy would realise that, while at the same time hoping it might not be so. He had thought of reminding Desmond that Cathy did not want to move, and even asking him why, if it wasn't about money, he had pressed for the move. Cathy wasn't short of money; enough, he guessed, to see her through. But there was a certitude in all of Desmond's positions. He had clear reasons for what he did. Desmond would shelter behind the mantra of Cathy's 'best interests' as everyone did 'out there' – always claiming to be an arbiter of what her best interests were. Just as the doctors and nurses, and welfare officers, and therapists, said that they were trained to know what was best, Desmond would say that, as a husband who had lived with this case for many years, he knew what was best. David knew he could never win the 'best interests' argument with Desmond or anybody else. If he asked Desmond why *what Cathy wanted* could not be considered part of her best interests, he would only elicit an unpleasant, curling lip.

Two days later, David was in the drive when Desmond pulled up in his car. David was enjoying the burst of colour from a row of freshly planted red geraniums. Desmond slammed to a halt in front of the porch. Poppy – of all animals – was in the back, jumping, and barking loudly. Desmond got out, and opened the door for Poppy, who leaped up at David.

"Here's the bloody dog, David! Look after it, while I see Helmut."

David was physically overwhelmed by Poppy, and by the oddity of Desmond himself bringing her to the Hall.

Helmut had already seen Desmond, and came out on to the porch in a pool of sunlight.

Desmond launched in before Helmut could speak.

"I'm giving the dog to you, Helmut, and good riddance!"

He spoke with irritable humour.

"But Mrs Temple?"

"I've taken it back from her. Given her a Labrador pup, instead."

"Ah, yes, but how much are you asking for Poppy?"

"It's a gift."

"This is very generous."

"It's not. I'm glad to get rid of the beast."

"Cathy will be so pleased."

"I haven't done it for Cathy. She'll be out of here soon, and the dog can't go with her. Not to London. She won't miss it anyway."

"Still, she'll be very happy at being able to see Poppy regularly ... while she's here," Helmut said diplomatically, not wanting to open a disagreement with his benefactor.

"I've done it because the dog's a pain in the neck. It's caused me no end of trouble. I'm sick of it. I thought I was doing the animal a favour in letting Mrs Temple have it. Since then it's caused nothing but complaints and arguments. If it wants to live here, let it!"

David could hardly grasp that his biggest problem could be solved so easily, and in a way that he would never have thought remotely possible. This solution was overshadowed by Cathy's imminent departure – everybody seemed to take it for granted that she would be going – but at least there would be a short period when Cathy and Poppy could enjoy each other. And his mind raced beyond this point. There might well be ways, particularly when he had greater freedom, to get Poppy to London, to see Cathy.

"Is Mrs Temple happy with … this?" David asked Desmond.

"David, she suggested it. Not the new Labrador puppy. That was a separate present from me to her. She said she'd been overwrought about the dog, and a bit mean, and she asked me to give it to Denby Hall."

David wanted to know what made Anita change her mind, but it was such an intimate question that he could only put it if he and Desmond were alone.

As Desmond handed Helmut an envelope containing Poppy's papers, he said, "You'll have noticed what a nauseatingly doggy bunch the English are, Helmut. We love the beasts. Beat your patients, by all means, but don't try beating the dog! Ha, ha!"

"I assure you, Poppy will be adored," Helmut said gravely, not seeing anything funny.

After lunch, David pushed Cathy along the cliff path with Poppy. The vast white sky seemed to touch the cliff edge. They were walking along the edge of the earth. The southerly wind, strong and warm, flattened the wild flowers in the tussock. David told Cathy she could see Poppy on most days, because Helmut had promised to bring Poppy with him, whenever he was working at Denby Hall.

26

Knowing that David now knew who Anita was, Desmond explained how he had met her. He seemed to realise that he had presented his ties to Cathy as though they were exclusive, and in doing so, had created a misleading picture.

"It's strange how friendships start, David. Friendships can lead us into chains, or into delights. I know you and Cathy were new kids, thrown together at Denby Hall. Your relationship is a happy accident.

"With Cathy and me, it was me pursuing Cathy. I did a little work in an advice centre in Camden, for a charity, 'sort out your life' advice – if only I'd known how screwed up my own would become! Cathy was doing her community work. The tenants she worked with were my customers, when their affairs were in a sufficient tangle. I saw Cathy at work. I liked her style. She was intelligent, talented, gentle, refined and quite classy, even with her McFisheries jacket. I chased her. There wasn't much of an element of chance in it. I made it happen.

"Now, the start I had with Anita was quite different, and entirely a matter of chance. The thread of us getting to know each other was spun so thin it could have parted at any point in the first weeks, or months, or even the early years.

"Anita and I were brought together twenty years ago, by a waitress in a railway cafeteria. I had been to visit a factory in Brighton, owned by a client. I had a few minutes before catching the train to return to London. It was about 4pm, and I walked into the cafeteria at the station to get a cup of tea. I was served reluctantly by the waitress who banged the cups and muttered about closing. I realised I had overlooked the 'closed' sign partially hidden at one side of the doorway. I apologised, and took my cup to one of the nearby tables.

"A minute or so later, I looked up to see a blond woman a few years younger than me, about thirty, in a tan business suit, standing at the counter. Shapely. Smart. Stylish. Not one of the anorak brigade, like Cathy. A completely different sort of woman. She, too, had failed to see the sign. The waitress had now emerged from behind the counter and was sweeping the floor. I heard the waitress say to the blond woman, 'You're too late. We're closed.'

'Not in the middle of the afternoon, surely?'

'We've been going since six this morning, and we have to clean up. We're closed for an hour.'

'I only want a cup of tea.'

"The blond woman was standing in front of an automatic dispenser.

'Too bad,' the waitress said, sweeping an ever increasing wave of litter, in a cloud of dust, towards the door.

'I'm not asking you to do anything except take the money. I can work the vending machine.'

'No. We're closed.'

'I'll just put the money on the counter…' the blond woman said, reaching for a cup and positioning it under the spigot.

'Closed is closed,' the waitress said, thrusting the pile of dust and biscuit wrappers threateningly.

"The blond woman rested her bag on the counter, her back to me. I heard the surprise announcement of the London train on the loudspeaker. It was actually an earlier train, which was late. I began to walk out of the cafeteria. As I passed the blond woman, I said, 'Service isn't a word in her vocabulary.'

"She turned to me, laughed, and we both walked toward the platform, commiserating on the well-known difficulties of buying a cup of tea, and a cake, on the railway. We both entered the same carriage, which was nearly empty, and it seemed quite natural to sit together.

'Do you mind?' I asked, and she could hardly say no, but I thought she was pleased.

"Our pleasantries could easily have ended when we boarded the train, or she or I could have shown the intention of taking a separate seat, but none of these things happened.

"I found out later that Anita had noticed me earlier with one of the city councillors, who happened to be on the board of my client company. He had given me a lift to the station in his car. This connection served as a reference for me. I wasn't just any man Anita had met accidentally. I had connections with a respectable local politician.

"We were able to talk on the train as strangers sometimes do, rather distantly and objectively about our lives, laying out the big points. Anita told me she was married, and had her own business as an optician. She served on a trade association for opticians, hence her visit to London. Her husband was a history teacher, who was absorbed in collecting antiques and paintings. I explained that I was a design engineer, married for the second time with a wife in poor health, and two children from a previous marriage.

"What emerged from our mutual confidences, was the flavour that we each had marriages that were less than satisfactory. A commonplace situation, David. Perhaps even a stereotype. We were still talking as the train drew into Victoria, and it didn't seem impertinent to suggest that we might meet at some time for lunch. I suppose my precise motive was to take this woman to bed. I didn't think I was a womaniser, but I was sexually frustrated. Cathy's sexual relationship with me had long since dwindled away. And I was disappointed in the way my marriage was working in lots of small, inexpressible ways. I didn't understand what was happening. It might have been my fault. At that point, the really serious problems with Cathy were far in the distance. But that's how my affair with Anita began; trivially. And it was I think for both of us at that time, merely an attraction between two slightly discontented people, which would flare, and fade, in weeks or months.

"But this feeble thread survived. Indeed, it has thickened over the years to become a veritable steel cable."

27

When the expectation became an official reality, and it was confirmed to Cathy that she was going to another home, instead of the expected tantrum, she took the news quietly. The understanding might have seeped into her consciousness over a few days.

Cathy had a visit by two strange nurses from the new home, a man and a woman, to assess transport problems. Keith said 'they stood over her as though they were measuring her for a coffin.' Rose made encouraging remarks to Cathy about how 'lovely' the new home would be. Helmut told Cathy that he wanted her to stay, but there was nothing he could do. When Keith asked Cathy if she understood she was going, she simply nodded, and gave a quiet groan.

Cathy's manner, and even her appearance, changed in this period. She became withdrawn and stony. Even the prospect of playing the Freddie Mercury disc received no visible acknowledgment. She held on to Poppy more tightly when David was wheeling her in the grounds. He noticed that her neck had shrunk, and become veiny. The skin on her face was grey and drawn, emphasizing the squareness of her forehead, and the hollows in her cheeks. Her clouded eyes were yellow.

The doctor, nurses, and care staff, were very pleased with Cathy's lack of reaction, but David thought that she looked shocked, so shocked that she couldn't give a sign.

Keith made an announcement about Cathy's departure,

in the dining room, when all the residents were seated before lunch. He stood on a chair, and hushed everybody.

"I'm sorry to tell you, Cathy's going to be moved to another home in the next couple of weeks. We're all going to miss her, and we're going to send her off after a big party."

The residents were delighted at the prospect of a party, and there were genuine murmurs of regret from the less introverted. Cathy's dignity had earned her respect, despite her inability to communicate, and there were still a few residents who remembered the time when she could talk, sing, and play the piano, and who held one-sided conversations with her, filling in her answers themselves.

The residents began to work in the art class on the preparation of personal cards, and one huge best wishes card, eighteen inches high, which everybody would sign, or make their mark on. The selection of presents for Cathy began. These would be small, soft toys from the personal collections of the residents; sweets and chocolate (although Cathy could not eat them); scarves and small broaches, badges, and strings of beads. A special menu was to be prepared in the kitchen by Sally, and a cake with icing, and four candles to show the years Cathy had been at the Hall (it was nearly four). A whole programme of songs, speeches, and personal items began to be rehearsed. John Murdoch and Marlene, one of the care assistants, were coordinating all the efforts, and rehearsing the participants.

David expected to play the piano for a sing-song, but other than making a personal goodbye card, he avoided the enthusiastic preparations. He was cast into gloom by the prospect of Cathy's departure, although he concealed his feeling from her. He promised Cathy that he would get leave from Denby Hall, and bring Poppy to London to see her, as soon as he could.

When Desmond was recounting to David his life with Anita, he was rueful, not in the sense that he regretted the relationship, but as a man who now had a wide overview of it, and could see its inevitable failings, and what it might have been.

"Several years ago, Anita and I thought we should establish our own home. Somewhere we could be, other than hotels, seaside cottages, and on trips abroad. We were like gypsies, always on the move, always in strange beds in unknown places. Anita is a homely woman, and her head was full of plans, colours, and furnishing materials for our nest. She had a dream of cooking exquisite meals, which we would have tête à tête. We'd be cabinned up together in warmth and security. We might invite the odd friend, to whom we felt we could disclose our relationship, but that part of the dream was more hazy.

"We chose Horsham because it was conveniently between London and Brighton, and equally accessible to us both. We arranged to spend a weekend there, looking for a house or apartment to buy. We had booked the Charters Hotel which wasn't cheap, a supposedly comfortable, and quiet lodging, according to a tourist office brochure. As soon as I saw it, my spirits sank. It was on a backstreet, but a very busy one, thundering with traffic noise. The front of the building was almost unrecognisable from the elegant Victorian structure in the brochure. On a closer look, it was the same building, obscured by a clutter of signs and notices, and covered with a heavy pall of dust.

"Anita and I, arriving from different towns, met in the car-park, and I could see that she was glancing about, having doubts too. We checked in together. Perhaps the interior would be better. We had travelled so much together, that we had an automatic check-list of the items which can go wrong and make a stay miserable. Like being next to the machine room, or being kept awake by the airconditioning fans.

"We found that our room was on the rear ground floor, looking out on to the garbage bins. The room was dark and deep, and had a brass, four-poster bed. The rudimentary bathroom hadn't seen redecoration in perhaps fifty years. A new, plastic shower cabinet stood in a corner, like a telephone kiosk. The bedroom was filled with large pieces of unmatched Victorian furniture, a frowning mahogany wardrobe, a walnut dresser and a sprawling dressing table. Framed prints of faded girls in floral dresses were on the walls. The four poster bed had a pink and white floral cover, with piles of matching cushions. The floor had two different carpets with busy, unmatched designs. It was all pretentious, woefully shabby, and a disappointing backdrop for a weekend which might redefine our lives.

"Anita looked at me, and without speaking, we were communicating a reluctant agreement that the room was awful, and we never would have chosen it, had we known, but it would have to do. The effort of changing the room, which might lead to something worse, or finding another hotel, wasn't worth it. We didn't want our important mission sidetracked.

"Anita is the organiser, the maker of lists, and the keeper of schedules of activity. I willingly fit in. We decided to have another fifteen minutes in bed, and then go out for afternoon tea, or a beer, and finally to business, a tour of the estate agents' offices.

"After we left the hotel, we found our way along several blocks to the town centre. I saw nothing attractive in our short walk. A core of buildings went back a hundred years, the church, civic buildings and banks. The rest was shops, offices and department stores. The place was jaded, and sent no signals announcing itself as 'our' town.

"We went into a pub, and set up a couple of lagers by the fireplace. The pub smelled of dogs, but the beer was good. We had been talking a lot with our eyes, and were both left rather flat. In half an hour, we were outside again, moving between the windows of estate agents' shops. Sometimes we went in to enquire about properties displayed in the windows. I was more reticent than Anita. She questioned those agents we talked to, closely. But eventually we accepted that there wasn't a house that we want to look at more closely.

"We changed our tack, and walked around the perimeter of the town by the river, or was it a canal? One or two new blocks of apartments had been built here, and there was a large complex under construction. We wandered though a show-apartment, and studied the blocks from outside.

'One of the third floor apartments might be OK,' Anita said.

"I agreed. OK. Merely OK.

"We wanted to set up our own little cabin, and OK wasn't good enough. Anita felt the same. She didn't have to say it. We trudged on, trying to find a good position. We talked of views, of light, of storage space, of service charges, parking facilities. We found nothing interesting. The highest accolade was 'OK' and that wasn't high enough.

"Anita had been really excited when we set out from the hotel, the prospect of buying our own home, and ending this succession of foreign beds. And she had so many ideas for furnishing. She said her thoughts had been keeping her awake at night, and when she wanted to escape the cares of the day, she concentrated on the pleasure of creating our own space. Anita said that Eccleston Street, elegant as it was, wasn't her home; it was her husband's home, full of his antiques and paintings, positioned just as he wished.

"Our search that day was a cold, and tiring experience. The chill seemed to come up through the pavement. We decided to have dinner and talk it over. We canvassed the main streets, but found only fast food shops. The only restaurant we could find with tablecloths was closed. We settled for the Slug and Lettuce, a pub that promised a food menu, and chose soup of the day, and lamb chops, as the least repulsive items.

'Have we made a mistake in coming here?' Anita asked.

'Yes,' I said, 'I think we have.'

'But it's not only this place, Desmond, horrible as it is, it's …any place.'

'I didn't think about it very clearly,' I said, but the insight Anita had, was floating at the back of my mind too. 'We're not going to be able to see each other any more than we do now, even with an apartment or house here'

'Or somewhere else,' Anita added.

"In all our discussions, David, the importance of this obvious point hadn't come through, or had we pushed it aside, not wanted to recognise it? We'd both been yearning to make an imagined future into the present. We hadn't thought how valuable the real present was, limited as it was. Horsham's inhospitability had cleared our minds. Now, both of us were moving against anything that abridged the kind of present we shared.

'It's true,' Anita said. 'We meet on every opportunity we have already, and now I think of it, I don't want to limit our weekends in France, and our walks in the Dales, in favour of sitting in front of the television in a miserable little town somewhere…however snug our bolt hole.'

"Anita had injected, rather late in the day, the sharp dose of practicality we needed. The planner in her was overruling the homemaker. We both escaped our other lives as often as possible. But we did what we saw as our duties. We were both duty-ridden. As the years had passed, it was less and less thinkable that we could cut and run together. The cords which bound us to our spouses, had tightened rather than slackened. Up to the time Cathy went into Denby Hall, her need for my attention increased enormously. I couldn't devote less time to her. And how could Anita, by absenting herself from home more often, threaten her own carefully constructed small town reputation, and the placid and protected world of her husband? For her, the task of changing, or demolishing her marriage relationship became all the more awesome with every year. In any responsible sense, we were locked into a kind of quadrangle. Time together was a scarce commodity, and one that could not be enlarged.

"We finished the evening at the Slug and Lettuce with a second bottle of watery Cotes du Rhone. I felt a numb resignation as we walked back to the dingy hotel room, and the four poster bed."

28

Cathy's going-away party was held on Monday, at lunchtime. Lunch was the main meal of the day. The tables in the   dining room were rearranged to make a u-shape, with a seat of honour for Cathy in the centre. They were set with coloured cloths, table napkins and a paper hat for every place. Streamers and paper lanterns were hung across the room. On one side, a table was piled with brightly wrapped presents from the staff and residents, and the giant best wishes card, made by two of the residents and signed by everybody. The old piano had been pushed in from the sitting room, and stood against the wall.

The lunch started with a toast in rasberry juice by Helmut, made in an atmosphere of suppressed excitement.

"Cathy, I vant to say, on behalf of staff and residents, that we are sorry you are leaving. We know that you will be well looked after in your new home, and we wish you every happiness there. You have been with us more than three years, and we have come to know and love you. To Cathy!"

Helmut raised his glass high, and those who could stand, sprang to their feet. "To Cathy!"

Cathy sat imperiously in her privileged seat, while one of the carers gave her sips of juice from her non-spill mug.

John Murdoch remained on his feet when the others sat.

"I want to add a few words to those of our esteemed managing director," he said, pulling a sheaf of notes from his waistcoat pocket, and squinting at them. "Cathy, we know that the bosses have ordained that you must go, against your will, to a place that must, by definition, be inferior to the perfection of this establishment…"

Ian, the duty shift manager stood up clapping, "Thank you, John, thank you. Speeches and personal items will come later. Cook's ready to serve."

Amid a small spray of clapping, Ian put his hand on John's shoulder, and pressed him gently back into his chair. Helmut left the room with a wave of his hand, as the volume of the babble began to rise.

"Come on, everybody," Rose shouted, putting on a paper hat.

The residents put on their paper hats. Carrot soup was served, followed by roast chicken with roast potatoes, pumpkin, cabbage and thick gravy. The food was consumed with noisy gusto. The last course was jelly and ice-cream. Cathy's pureed version of each course was spooned into her mouth by Rose, who never usually did such tasks. Sally the cook, and a helper, carried in two huge rainbow sponges with vanilla icing, and one had four candles. There were loud cheers, while Rose neatly performed the trick of asking Cathy to blow out the candles, and then blew them out herself. Cream sponge was a special treat, and there were only a few crumbs left when it had been shared out.

While the staff discreetly cleared the tables, Ian took the floor to hand over the goodbye card, and preside over the unwrapping of the presents, one by one, with announcements of the names of the donors, usually to much whistling and hooting. Cathy appeared to watch, as a pile of soft toys, costume jewellery, and toiletries grew on the table in front of her.

"Now, Cathy," Keith said, "some of the staff and residents are going to perform a few items for you. They've all been practicing hard, and this will be better than a floor show in

Las Vegas! First, Barney, with a bit of Shakespeare."

When Keith sat down, David whispered to him, "Have you ever been to Las Vegas?"

"Never, mate. Wish I had."

Barney Colas recited the sonnet, *Let me not to the marriage of true minds Admit impediments. Love is not love which alters when it alteration finds.* Barney had worked hard, and found words that David could recall from the darkness. The audience enjoyed hearing the poem. It touched well known chords, like the songs David played, or a famous hymn, and as with many of those tunes and hymns, seemed to reach for the unattainable.

Two members of staff, Maggie and Paula, sang a duet, *Now is the Hour,* which David found sad. But the audience hummed, and swayed lightheartedly through the song. Mark Demeter restored hearty laughter with a conjuring trick that went wrong. About to show that he could retrieve, from the shuffled pack, a card that his audience knew, but he ostensibly did not, he fumbled and dropped the pack on the floor. The whistling and the stamping of feet was fierce. Mark gave up, thrusting his fist high above his head, like a footballer who has scored a goal.

David sat down at the piano, and everybody joined in a loud sing-song: *Pack Up Your Troubles, Tavern in the Town, When Irish Eyes are Smiling* and *Coming Round the Mountain.* When David had been through his repertoire, he played a compact disc of Queen's 'Bohemian Rhapsody' on the old stereo system. As the last words of the melody, *Nothing really matters to me,* were sung in Freddie Mercury's pure, imperative voice, Cathy's eyes glistened, and she struggled as if to speak.

In the lull, Keith appeared with Poppy.

"Now quiet everybody! Too much noise, and we'll have Helmut down here, and I'll get hell," he said in a loud voice. "We're going to have a group photo."

Cathy was wheeled out from behind the table, into the centre of the floor. Poppy sat on her hind quarters beside Cathy, seeming to understand the need for calm, although her tail never stopped beating the floor. The residents and staff gathered behind Cathy, all grins, and paper hats askew. Keith wise-cracked with everybody as he took the shots. Then Keith led Poppy toward the door, pushing through those residents who wanted to touch Poppy as though she was a talisman.

"Now we're going to have a dance, to end Cathy's party," Rose said, as care assistants moved some of the tables out of the way.

Dancing was a regular event at Denby Hall, enjoyed by almost every resident, and the staff. Cathy, accompanied by Rose, took her place on the floor ahead of everybody else. David seated himself at the piano again, and pounded out his flawed versions of favourites like *Goodnight Irene* and *Home on the Range*. Everybody else was dancing in pairs, trios, foursomes or alone. Some pushed a wheelchair-bound resident from behind, some leaned over the front of the chair, resting their arms on the armrests, moving the chair in time to the music.

After twenty minutes, David was sweating and tired. He switched on the stereo for those who were left, and took Cathy upstairs in the lift. The presents, and the card, were in two bulging plastic bags, hooked over the handles of the wheelchair.

In her room, Cathy refused a Freddie Mercury recording. "Do you want me to go?"

Cathy made a 'no' noise, and David sat on the bed for a while, his hand on hers. Cathy was wide awake, staring ahead, occasionally turning her head to him, and then away. In profile, with her hair drawn back, tied at the crown, and plaited, she looked regal as the shadows deepened in the room. Churning clouds were overhead, and it was going to shower. Before them, tumbled on the bed, were the presents, and the farewell card. The card was covered in scribbled drawings, verses, and short comments, as well as signatures. It had a big red heart, with a red ribbon, glued on the front.

David left Cathy after more than half an hour, and found Rose. He said he thought Cathy looked ill.

"I'm not surprised, after what she had today," Rose said.

Rose and David went to Cathy's room. She was calm. Rose took her pulse.

"You're fine, aren't you darling? You've had a lovely, lovely party," Rose said.

"She's not fine," David said.

"Bit of indigestion. I think she's all right, but I'll get Dr Floor," Rose said, frowning at David.

Dr Floor arrived half an hour later. He felt Cathy's pulse, and took her blood pressure.

"Probably excitement. The party. Blood pressure's a bit high. Bed now. I'll see her in the morning."

After the care assistants had washed Cathy, and put her to bed, David went to her room. She was lying on her back, with her eyes open. The high sides of the bed were up – a safety precaution – so she was lying in a padded box. He asked her whether she wanted him to sit with her a while, and she indicated, yes. She refused any music. David stayed until it was dark, and she closed her eyes.

29

The night after the party, David could not sleep. He had eaten too much cream cake. For him, the party was not a joyful event, although he had taken a leading part. He had tried to give the appearance of enjoying himself. He wanted Cathy to have a cheery send-off, but it was marred by his own feeling of impending loss. And his concern about the pain the move would inflict upon Cathy. Keith's image of the sixth floor cell remained in his mind.

One touch of brightness, now that the tussle over Poppy had been resolved, was the possibility of a visit to London to see Cathy. He was determined that he would manage this somehow. He was fairly sure Cathy understood his plan, but she was unmoved. And he found Cathy's attitude towards leaving unnerving. The proposal had turned her to stone. These thoughts, and the indigestion, kept him awake.

David heard the sounds of a disturbance down the corridor about two am, low cries and calls of consternation, possibly from staff. The night shift care assistants were climbing the stairs on the thin carpet, and the lift clattered. A vehicle scrunched on the drive. He had not drawn the blinds, and the windows were spotted with rain. A green coloured light, flashing from the vehicle outside, lit the globules of rain on the glass, and blazed on the wall of his room. He got out of bed, and looked down from the window. It was the emergency doctor's car.

He went to the door of his room. He saw a huddle of

people, cases of equipment, and a stretcher at the end of the corridor. He could not tell for certain, but a kind of gnawing inside told him that the huddle was around Cathy's room.

He pulled on his dressing gown, and waited in his own doorway, listening, for a long time. People were still in the corridor, but very quiet. He wanted to go down there, and see for himself, but he feared to do so. He would be sent back to bed very sharply if he was seen by staff. Eventually, the people ebbed away taking their stretchers and bags with them, and only the usual night lights remained on in the empty corridor.

Now he ventured down the corridor. Yes, he could see as he approached, that the door of Cathy's room was open, and the light on. He looked in. Maggie was sitting in a chair by the bed where Cathy lay. The side panels had been removed. Maggie sensed him, and looked up.

"Gawd y' frightened me, David. What y'aboot at this hour!"

"Cathy?"

"Och, the pur wee thing's gone."

They both looked at what David had first thought was a sleeping figure. It was Cathy, on her back, the bedclothes smoothed over her arms and chest, her head visible, and surrounded by the wild rush of hair that had been released from her hair band. Her eyes were closed. The tension and worry, which had pitted her face since she had been told she would be moved, was gone. Her skin was shiny, smooth, and almost transparent.

"She looks… peaceful," he said.

"Yes, she was peaceful. She never really became conscious, as far as we know. She struggled a little, and then gave up."

"Can I stay a while?"

"You shouldn't really, David… I know she was your friend."

David sat down in a chair next to Maggie. He felt a deep blow, but no shock or surprise. His plan to see Cathy in London was really a fantasy. What had happened tonight had started weeks or months ago, when the initiative to move Cathy was only an idea. The idea had swelled into the gradual ordering of events by many people. The idea gained substance, and force, always moving forward, and coming to the inevitable conclusion. There was no surprise. Only the heavy weight of the arrival of what was expected. David was a bystander who could see it all. Perhaps he was the only one who had a glimpse of the possibility that Cathy would not allow herself to be moved, and could not be moved, from Denby Hall.

The regime of 'no choice' was over.

Ian, the night supervisor, loomed out of the shadows behind him. "What are you doing here, young David?"

"Just…sitting."

"I think you should come back to your room with me. Maybe I can give you something to make you sleep."

"I don't want to sleep," David said, following Ian up the corridor, back to his room.

Ian turned in the doorway "OK, but don't think too much. Cathy was very ill."

David lay back on his pillow, and heard another vehicle arrive, lights flashing on the bedroom wall, voices, then the rumble of the elevator and more muted voices in the corridor.

His thought about Cathy was that at last the final brick had been placed in the wall of the cell around her; she was in perfect, soft darkness, and she didn't really mind.

In the morning, David was awake long before breakfast. He put on his dressing gown, waited until the corridor was clear of staff, and went back to Cathy's room. The door was closed.

He opened the door. The empty bed had been stripped to the mattress. The bedclothes had been removed. The dresser was clear. The wardrobe, with the doors hanging open, empty. The drawings, and cards, and notes, and coloured strings, and bells, that had been stuck on, or hung from the walls, had been taken down, except one home-made tinsel star near the door. The little bottles of lotion and perfume, useless gifts, which clustered on her shower-room shelf, had been removed with her toilet articles.

All Cathy's possessions were in three black plastic bags, leaning against the wall with her television set and radio-CD player beside them. David opened the black bags, and looked inside. Two were crammed with clothes.

In the other bag were the photographs of her family. Desmond, his son and daughter, the nephews and nieces who were never seen, the dead parents, with the faded postcards, all jumbled about, facing each other, and facing away from each other, in the darkness of the bag. Words written to a Cathy who couldn't read them, images of people and events that were, now that she was gone, meaningless.

He saw the ragged bundle of love letters, packed into the dark clutter. He thought of the passion behind the blurred handwriting, in a foreign language, which had come across the Atlantic Ocean, and perhaps been returned by a gentle young woman. A couple had faded away, across miles of implacable ocean. Now only a bundle of paper, in a black bag.

Keith caught David in the act, as he was rushing past the open door.

"Whoa, David! Ian put it in the book that you were here last night. She's gone, man, but at least she had her party."

"Do not resuscitate," David said.

"That was Cathy's choice."

"She had no choice."

"Whaddya mean?" Keith said, cuttingly.

David wanted to speak, but he couldn't find suitable words. He wanted to say that Cathy had been unhappy about *Do not resuscitate*, but the forces 'out there' were irresistible. David wasn't sure Keith would understand, well meaning as he was.

"What... happened?"

"A stroke. Now you go back to your room, get dressed, and go down to breakfast."

David stood still. He could see in the wall mirror, that his plump cheeks were pale, and the usual tiny lines of good nature, which gathered around his mouth and eyes, had gone. He met Keith's wide-open, receptive gaze with silence.

"OK, David. Stay here if you want. What the hell is breakfast anyway? We have one every day of our lives."

30

David didn't know what happened about Cathy's funeral, but he assumed Desmond arranged it privately. However, Rose, who had never attended church in all the time that David had known her, decided that a memorial service should be held at St Giles in Ponsonby Road. Rose said that Cathy had been with them at one moment, and gone the next, and there had to be what she called a 'closure.'

"I mean," she said, "we all expected to see Cathy at breakfast the night after her party, and she wasn't there. It's unfinished business. Just gone, *pfffft*, leaving no trace."

This seemed to be a powerful argument with Helmut, the staff, and most of the residents, although Mark, John and David were confused about what a closure was, and whether one was necessary. However, they were in accord that the service would be an agreeable outing. It would be good to hear a tribute to Cathy. It did not seem to David to be an insuperable obstacle that Cathy, at least in her later months, had not liked going to St Giles.

Desmond readily agreed to play the principal role, and invitations were sent out to members of the family, and a scattering of people who had known Cathy at the Hall, volunteers, patients' representatives, ex-care assistants and therapists. Rose had a particular feeling for Cathy, and she worked with dedication on the project. Rose had lost a husband to heart failure, and a daughter to cancer. She was beyond family illness now, in the clear water of other people's illnesses, ignoring her own painful hip, and varicose veins.

Desmond called in at the Hall to see Rose about the preparations, and made a point of finding David. They talked in the garden. Desmond, in good humour, said that death had a way of inveigling relations and acquaintances out of their hiding places. True to his comment, the response to the invitations was surprisingly complete. Cathy's brother and sister accepted with a sprinkling of nephews and nieces, as did Cathy's stepchildren, Mike and Sandra, and a host of people who had known Cathy before they left Denby Hall.

Desmond suggested to David that as he was Cathy's best friend, he might like to play the piano or say a few words. Desmond said he would arrange for a piano to be available. At first, David refused, scared of performing before such an audience, but when he had an opportunity to think it over, he decided he should do it for Cathy. Desmond also mentioned that he had felt obliged, purely as a matter of form, to ask Cathy's brother and sister if they wanted to play a part and, after some sniffing, Simon had accepted.

"What a bloody nerve!" Desmond said. "That's where politeness gets you."

Desmond had a deep and unconcealed resentment of Simon and Denise, but he had, at least, the comfort that he had managed to exclude them from Cathy's will – a step that Cathy had described to David as "a small act of vindictiveness, which Desmond considered necessary, and which I hadn't the strength to resist."

David was troubled by Desmond's observation about death. He saw people coming out of dark cracks, and corners, people who had largely ignored Cathy over recent years. Why should they want to go to the memorial service? He couldn't understand it.

On the day, all but the skeleton staff at Denby Hall, and

the few patients who were totally immobile, attended. It was a happy event. The old hymns were belted out by the organist, and the congregation sang joyfully. St. Giles, full of flowers, let in some rays of sunshine through its grimy lead-light windows, and seemed to perk up. At Desmond's request, the vicar played the role of master of ceremonies only.

Desmond was a smooth and effortless speaker, who delivered his words with careful inflections, and without a note. He gave a warm eulogy of Cathy's achievements, from leading lady in HMS Pinafore as a schoolgirl, head prefect of the Troon Academy, scholar at Edinburgh University, volunteer worker in the Amazon, community worker in London, to accomplished amateur landscape painter, musician and singer.

When he referred touchingly to the woman he loved, David thought Desmond meant the talented person, who had slipped away almost unnoticed many years before, rather than the silent Egyptian princess, who had recently been sealed in her cell. Cathy would, of course, have said that there was no talented person who slipped away years ago; that Desmond's words were just so many images of her 'self' in the eyes of others, a bundle of fleeting impressions, an imaginary snapshot.

For David's item, he went to the microphone, without having thought through what he might say. Whenever he had tried to prepare himself in the preceding days, his mind had slewed away from the subject as too depressing.

"Cathy was my best friend, and I want to play something for her," was all he managed.

At least these words came without hesitation, and he went to the piano, and played *We'll Meet Again*. As he played, some classical embellishments came back to him. The song disturbed the audience. Some people sang in an undertone, some sobbed. It seemed to take a long time before the effect of the song had passed away, and the service could continue.

At the same time, David couldn't see how their spirits *could* meet again, but the thought that they might was pleasing to him, and everybody else in the church. You never want to say goodbye, and the song held out a possibility that you didn't have to.

Cathy's brother stepped up to the podium looking compact in his dark suit, green light flashing on his rimless spectacles. He spoke of a childhood by the sea at Brancaster, with his two sisters; fancy dress parties; their adventures in an old sailing boat on the Norfolk Broads, and picnics with jam sandwiches, in the orchard at the bottom of the garden.

The service ended with a thunderous rendering of Blake's *And did those feet in ancient time.*

Desmond caught up with David as they were coming out of St. Giles, and led him off the path, to an area with long grass, and old, broken tombstones sticking up at all angles like World War II tank traps.

"We've got a couple of minutes, and I want to talk to you, David. I know you spoke to Graham Temple."

"I'm sorry ... I only wanted to make arrangements for Poppy."

"You don't give up easily."

"I thought Mr Temple knew that you and Anita were friends," David said.

"Look, you did me a good turn. No, Graham Temple didn't know about Anita and me. Anita had kept it from him all these years. But the connection of our names was enough to lift the corner of the mat, and his suspicions crawled out. It was undeniable, I suppose. That was the end of twenty years of deceit."

David clenched his teeth in dismay at what he had triggered.

"What about Mr Temple?"

Desmond sat on a tombstone looking pleased, his black, usually imploring eyes, hooded under his eyelids. He adjusted the cuffs of his shirt, so that they protruded an inch below the sleeve of his suit, the gold links showing.

"I'll tell you, David, because I don't want you to feel involved or responsible. After Anita had hounded you out of the house – which, by the way, she was very sorry about afterwards, because it wasn't your fault – I mean, you didn't know – Graham and Anita naturally had one hell of an argument."

Desmond explained how shocked Graham Temple was. The revelation had descended upon him like the smashing of his precious Ming dynasty vase. How could his total ignorance have persisted for so many years? Anita and Graham fought verbally amongst the chips of the vase Anita had thrown at David, and the contents of her shopping bags spilled on the rug. She was concerned that Graham was going to collapse. He was pale, and draped feebly in his chair, like a man about to have a heart attack.

'Talk to me!' he croaked. 'Tell me, woman!'

'All right, then. It's true,' she said. 'I've been seeing Desmond Marsden ever since...'

'Ever since the randy bastard came sniffing around our marriage decades ago.'

'Yes. Our life together was already dead or dying then, I don't know why.'

'Because you were a frigid bitch.'

'Do you want to talk about that stuff?'

'I repelled you, did I?'

'Perhaps it wasn't as strong as that. The spark died. It's no use analysing it now.'

'It died because somebody else was fucking you!'

'No, before that.'

'Why didn't you tell me? Why go on?'

Anita paused, troubled by the hurtful truth. 'Desmond couldn't leave his wife.'

'It's all about Desmond is it? What he could or couldn't do!'

'No, it's all about Cathy Marsden. Desmond couldn't do anything because she couldn't do anything. She's dominated our lives, Desmond's, mine, even yours.'

'So I was the default choice,' he murmured, putting his hands over his face.

'*And* I stayed because I thought we might come right. If I was an unsatisfactory partner, why didn't *you* leave *me*?' Anita asked.

'Because *I* thought we might come right! What an idiot I was.' Graham had a bitter smile.

'So we both had hopes that have come to nothing,' she said, trying to calm him.

'It's the utter disloyalty, the gross breach of the trust I placed in you. Years and years of lies and deceit. You've said you were going to 'commercial conferences' as the opticians' bigwig, and instead you were sodding about with Marsden in a grotty little pension in Toulouse.'

'Don't hype it up, Graham. You've had a nice, cosy life following your own pursuits, your historical societies, your paintings and antiques. You've shut me out. I've been here to keep house. Look at this place. Look at the furniture, the paintings, the rugs. It's you, you, you!'

'You'd have to admit that my taste is rather better than yours.'

'Even at a time like this, you can't resist a jibe, can you, Graham? It's one of your lovable qualities. I meant you could replace me with a housekeeper tomorrow, and hardly notice it.'

'So you've been sustaining Desmond Marsden, as it were, while he looked after his ailing wife, for all these years.'

'I suppose that's true. *And* I've sustained you in the manner you have chosen, the nominal wife and servant. Never a partner, and never a friend.'

'I see. I owe my nominal marriage to the disabled Catherine Marsden. Her husband can't leave her and run away with you, so you can't run away from me. This poor innocent lady is the lynch pin.'

'It's true.'

'What a nasty little foursome we are!'

Desmond found the story amusing. "The point, David, is that Anita has been fluffing about for the last few years, agonising over whether to leave Graham and move in with me. She's a good woman. He is frail, and she really believed she owed him, so she hung on. I don't think she could ever handle the fact that the deception had become so monstrous. I mean, all those years, and the easiest way was to let it go on. Anyway, Graham made her mind up. So she lives with me now."

"What about Mr Temple?"

David could see that he had unwittingly unlocked the quadrangle, as Desmond had called it once. Now that Cathy had gone, Desmond and Anita were preening themselves, and Graham Temple was pushed to one side.

"Ah, yes, Graham. Poor old Graham," Desmond said, "It's a not-so-merry-go-round, isn't it? Now, at last, Graham is the loser. That's the way it is."

David had Cathy's vision of the Anita-Graham creature, always partially blind and crippled, always unable to communicate vital messages from one half of its brain to the other, giving up the struggle for life.

"Forget your part in it, David. You're as innocent as Poppy," Desmond said, getting up and putting his arm around David's shoulders, and squeezing him warmly. "You've been a very good friend, and helpmate to me."

"Do you want Poppy back now?"

"No, no, no. Don't be ridiculous. Indeed, I'll send Helmut a cheque that will cover a truckload of dog-food!"

Afternoon tea and refreshments, including sherry for those non-residents who wanted it, were served in the St. Giles' church hall, on the other side of Ponsonby Road, after the ceremony, at Desmond's expense. David was confused at the implications of the service, and unable to accept Desmond's view that he was free of blame. He lost himself in the crowd, drifting from one knot of people to another. He was pleased that Anita and Desmond were happy, but worried that Mr Temple, obviously, was not.

Desmond materialised before David, with his hand familiarly on the arm of a bulging-eyed man, in his late twenties. Desmond introduced his son, Mike.

"I've heard of you from Dad," Mike said abruptly, shaking hands.

"I've heard of you … from Cathy."

"Thanks for looking after my step-mother."

It sounded very proprietorial, 'my stepmother.'

"Why did you come today?" David asked, the words coming out this time, before he had a chance to reflect on their implications.

"To support my father," was the quick, almost rehearsed reply.

David knew that if he asked why Mike hadn't supported his father by coming to see Cathy occasionally, he would receive a clear, and probably unpalatable answer. Mike, according to Cathy, was the sort of unsentimental person who knew precisely what he was doing, and why. Perhaps that was one clue to how he made his millions. Cathy had been very placid about her relationship with Mike and his sister, Sandra. She said she had never tried to mother them. She wasn't capable of it. Cathy had reckoned that there was an in-built, almost impersonal, alienation from a stepmother, with stepchildren in their teens – simply, that their father's choice of a mate, wasn't *their* mother.

Desmond had moved away. Mike and David bared their teeth at each other in attempted grins. Mike, shot his head round quickly, at a variety of angles, to see who was near, and moved away too.

Soon, Desmond was at David's shoulder again. "This is Cathy's sister, Denise."

Denise's features had been smeared by tears, and reddened like a piece of raw meat, set in a black basket of hair. She said how 'terribly, terribly awful' it was for everybody.

David didn't think it was like that at all. He could see a whole canvas that was supposed to be the colour of Cathy's life, being unfurled, and daubed by the occupants in the hall around him, in their choice of colours. Cathy was the focal point for memories about themselves. David was no nearer understanding why all these diverse people had come to the service; why they should want to dredge up here, the memories that connected them tenuously to Cathy, when they could do so in their own homes. There was even a comfortably padded Roman Catholic priest from Sao Paulo, who had worked with Cathy when she was in Manaus.

Paul Prosser was unobtrusively present, a friend and companion of Cathy's, whom David stood with for a time. Paul was slightly spaced out as usual. His speech had become slower in the last two years, and more hesitant, and his eyes were glassed in dark hollows. His manner hadn't changed. He was as light-hearted and convivial as always.

"What do you think of it, David?" he asked.

"I don't know … it's not much about Cathy."

"It can't be, can it? She's gone. It's people massaging

themselves, a kind of gentle public wanking ceremony, with sherry and scones."

"But nice," David said.

The din of voices was interrupted by the urgent ringing of a spoon on a glass. David looked in the direction of the sound, and saw John Murdoch, who was prone to use every possible opportunity to make a public speech, holding an arm up for attention. He was on the dais at the end of the hall. John, who had a half-full sherry glass in one hand, had escaped the keen-eyed supervision of Rose and the other carers. He was not permitted to drink alcoholic liquor.

"Distinguished guests, ladies and gentlemen, your attention please…"

David could see that Rose, Ian and Keith were alarmed, but also stilled, by the understanding that they were in a gathering with people from 'out there.'

"I want to propose a toast to Cathy's memory…"

John's poise and diction were at least as faultless as Desmond's, and the crowd stilled to hear what was only to be expected, an affectionate toast. Helmut now joined Rose, Keith and Ian and they conferred, quietly and anxiously. It wasn't a simple matter of easing John down from the platform, as they would have done at Denby Hall. After all, he hadn't said or done anything wrong – yet.

"We're here to celebrate the memory of a very special person… charge your glasses…" John said.

Under the cover of murmurs of approval from the audience, as they hustled to get their glasses full, David guessed that Helmut would be counselling a pause on the part of the Denby Hall managers. Uppermost in Helmet's mind would be how unseemly it would look if they moved against John.

"Let's remember Cathy for the beautiful person she was a few weeks ago…" John said, raising his glass.

Keith looked at Helmut, waiting for his signal. Keith was Denby Hall's doer, he was the one who would act. On command, he would calmly sweep John off the dais, and into the crowd. Helmut's wrinkled face was held up like a sensitive radar, waiting to receive and translate impulses from John.

"Let's not talk about jam sandwiches in the orchard …" John said, dropping his voice, and moving his head to eyeball the whole audience.

The notion of jam sandwiches sent a pleasurable ripple through the gathering. David thought that John had just about taken his speech to the limit, and that at any moment, for fear of what might come next, Helmut had to give the order. But Helmut, his cheeks quivering, held fire.

"Let's remember the real Cathy, who has recently left us, the gentle lady in a wheelchair…"

"To Cathy!" Barney Colas bawled, with perfect timing, as John's voice lowered.

"To Cathy!" the audience responded.

Everybody drank the toast, and John Murdoch voluntarily left the platform in a muted voicing of approvals, and clapping.

As they were easing out of the hall, David was close to Helmut, and he saw Simon Hurst claim Helmut's arm.

"Who was that man who spoke?" Simon barked, quite loudly.

"He was…" Helmut shied away from admitting that a resident had spoken.

"A friend of Cathy's," David interjected.

"Damn cheek of that man!" Simon said. "Who does he think he is? I'm *her brother*. I was about to propose a toast! I'll give him jam sandwiches!"

31

As David was passing the reception desk on the way upstairs, Kay said, "David, I had a call from a woman a few minutes ago, asking if you were in. She said she was going to call round. When I asked her name, she said she was going to surprise you."

Kay grinned flirtatiously. David didn't really know any girls, or women, as personal friends. Caroline Higgins would never approach him in this way. He thought it could be a previous care assistant who had now left, but he couldn't think which one. An hour later, he was lying on his bed listening to Simply Red, when Keith looked in.

"Guess who's downstairs asking for you?"

David hoisted himself up, with a feeling of pleasant anticipation.

"The bitch of Eccleston Street, Lady Temple!"

David swallowed hard, although her presence didn't alarm him. "I wonder what she wants?"

"I can get rid of her if you like," Keith said.

David thought of his awful conversation with Mr Temple. "No. It's something I'd better do."

"You're sure? Call me if you have any problems."

"Thanks ..." Unnerving thoughts about the police, the girl dog-walker and the broken vase swirled in his head, but he dismissed them.

"You know who she is?" Keith said, "I found out from Kay. She's one of the good and the great in the town.

Sometime local authority councillor, ex head of the WI, and the Townswomen's Guild, chair of this committee, head of that tribunal, a Justice of the Peace. You know? Mrs Big."

David had to adjust his image of Anita slightly. He had thought of her as a neglected, peripheral figure, at the edges of the lives of her husband and Desmond; a person who was neurotically waiting to live, rather than a career woman in her own right. He went downstairs to meet her in the lobby.

Anita had an uncertain smile. She did not frighten him. He felt at quite a distance from the concerns of people out there. They became agitated at events that seemed unimportant to him. Her hair was wet, and hung down in strings. She was wearing a belted white raincoat, which was short and showed off her tanned legs.

"I wanted to see you, David, if I can call you that …"

"C-come into the sitting room."

"Can we go for a walk? … The weather is terrible, but…"

Very quickly, he fetched an anorak, and Kay let them out. They picked their way along the soft cliff path. Anita Temple's delicate shoes were soon muddy, but she seemed not to notice. The rain was light, and there was no wind. The seaward side was a misty, pearl space. The roadway side was blotted out by fog. They walked in a capsule of privacy.

"I called Helmut, and apologised to him," she said. "All that stupid business about the police. I'm very sorry. But I wanted to see you personally. Desmond thinks you're terribly worried about the meeting you had with Graham…"

"I am."

"First, can I say I've been wrong all along about Justina … Poppy."

"It's OK, now. And thanks for agreeing to hand over Poppy."

"Now it's too late."

"No. Cathy never knew. She saw Poppy quite a few times."

Anita Temple stopped and looked at David. He couldn't tell whether the wet on her face was rain or tears. Her eyes were red, with shadows underneath.

"She never knew about me keeping Poppy away from her?"

"Nobody told Cathy. All she knew was… she saw Poppy occasionally."

Anita seemed to be satisfied with this. "I felt … so angry and frustrated. I can't tell you how Cathy has dogged us …"

"Dogged?" David couldn't help showing a flicker of amusement.

"I'm not blaming her, poor woman. She couldn't help herself. Poppy was the final stroke… do you understand, David?"

David nodded. He did understand. Cathy had described him once as being forgiving, like a priest. Anita needed to be absolved from her pettiness before she could rest. The truth was David didn't forgive Anita, any more than he forgave Cathy. He merely listened uncritically, and tried to learn.

"And about the scene at home – well it *was* home to me, before I left – when I threw the vase at you. I want to apologise to you about that."

"I wanted to see *you*, but Mr Temple tried to help…"

"Please don't worry … I was taken completely off-balance. I behaved … crazily."

"Desmond told me the vase was worth five thousand pounds."

Anita had no thought of vases. "Everything's changed now. For the better. As a result of that meeting, as Desmond told you…"

"What about Mr Temple?"

"Yes, I worry about him. I care for him. It was a terrible shock. Desmond says Graham's 'an obsessionally focussed loner'. He may be right, but it doesn't mean Graham isn't a good man in many ways. I mean, he may have had a few thoughts that we would part years ago, but ..." Anita suddenly stopped her excited charge.

"I'm talking too much, David. I suppose it's because you were in my life at an important moment."

"What will become of Mr Temple?"

"Oh, he's really a completely self-sufficient individual. The bruise to his pride will subside in time. He doesn't need me personally for anything."

David was uneasy at Anita's summary dismissal of Graham Temple. She had turned her back on him.

"Some good has come out of it, at least," David said.

"Oh, yes! I suppose that's selfish. I'm very happy. And you're the one who brought it about, David, although you never intended to!"

"You could say Poppy brought it about ... that's why I was at your house," he said.

But he thought, and could not mention to Anita, that you could also say, that in an indirect way, Cathy brought it about.

32

Three months after Cathy's death, David was judged fit to leave Denby Hall. He had no say in this decision. He tried to be as cooperative as he could. Caroline Higgins said he was becoming *institutionalised*. Although the word seemed to David to mean *enjoying life at Denby Hall*, to Caroline it was like a creeping disease, which would disable him further. The disease could only be halted by severing his connection with the place. Caroline's smooth face had a mask-like certainty on this subject.

Pat Harden, Denby Hall's social worker, had a routine discussion with David about his relocation. Pat knew from the files that he would be returning to his father's house in Somerset, and taking an information technology course in Bristol. They talked about the accommodation options for this. David said, by the way, that he would rather stay around the Denby Hall area for a while. When Helmut brought Poppy to Denby Hall, which was three, sometimes four days a week, he was able to walk her, and he was reluctant to give this up.

Pat seemed pleased that he had some thoughts of his own. "Well, let's have a look at the possibilities," she said. She mentioned that there were a couple of small, redecorated apartments coming up on the housing estate, and she thought that he might be able to get one of them. She said people who needed rehabilitation obtained some priority. With Pat's help, he applied for an apartment, on the understanding with her that he would arrange a local venue for his computer course.

One of his daily activities in the past six months, had been as a volunteer in the kitchen at Denby Hall. He didn't mind the messy work, and enjoyed helping to prepare the food, and learning a little of how the meals, for more than forty people, were assembled and cooked. Helmut heard that he was keen to stay in the vicinity, and he offered David a job in the kitchen for three hours a day, five days a week, for a small sum. Helmut made it clear that he would prefer that David had his father's agreement.

When David explained to his father, on the telephone, what he wanted to do, his father listened without comment, sighed, and said he would come down to Denby Hall. He arrived the next morning, looking worried. His father had apparently called Helmut, and the three met in Helmut's room.

David's father began with a head of steam directed at Helmut:

"It's monstrous, that after all the arrangements I've made for David's welfare, your social worker brushes them aside and arranges local accommodation, *so that David can walk a dog!*"

"Ah, walking a dog is good ... but it's not quite like that, Mr Thurgood," Helmut said.

"No. It's worse. You've offered David a job!"

"When David had made up his mind that he would like to stay," Helmut said, phlegmatically.

"You're cutting across everything David's psychotherapist, and I, have done."

"Knots can be untied, Mr Thurgood. David will have to decide," Helmut said affably.

"You're making it more difficult, Helmut."

"Giving him choices?"

David remained silent. His father fumed for a quiet moment, and then turned on him.

"I know you've enjoyed Denby Hall, David, but you have to break with a place like this. You're getting well now. It's not a place for well people."

"I'm not sure what well is," David replied.

"I am, my boy, believe me. Look, I'll tell you what I'll do by way of a compromise," his father said, regaining some of his usual amiability. "You want to be a chef? Not at all in line with your abilities, but all right, it's what you want to do. If you want to be a chef, I can get you a course with a Michelin star man in Bristol."

David's father gave a throaty chuckle, and gestured with his hands, as though he had performed a magic trick.

"This is a very valuable offer, David," Helmut said.

"I don't think I want to be a chef."

His father's face twitched. "But you said ... what *do* you want?"

"To work in the kitchen at Denby Hall."

"A kitchen hand?"

"Maybe, yes. I'll learn some cooking."

"A kitchen hand, oh no!"

"What's wrong with that?" David asked.

"David, you're refusing not one, but two great opportunities ... the IT training, and a course with a decent chef!" his father said, incredulously.

His father slapped his hand down hard on David's knee. The gesture was a surrogate for shaking David. He was causing a lot of worry. But the last few years had taught him that he had to speak from his side of the chasm.

"I know, and thanks, but..."

His father's patience had worn thin. "You haven't any ambition, have you?" he said, curtly.

The discussion ended there stiffly, and was followed by weeks of silence from his father. At last, he had a call from Caroline Higgins, saying that his father agreed with the employment at Denby Hall, as a temporary measure, but David should think carefully, and if he changed his mind, he should ring her immediately. David liked the kitchen hands at the Hall, and he was slowly learning to cook. He would also be able to continue to have lunch with Mark Demeter, and John Murdoch, and a new young woman at their table, Lorna, who had a raw hollow in her forehead from a motorcycle accident. Helmut said David was also welcome to continue to go to the Hall's current affairs meeting, and he wanted to go, just to be part of the group. He never listened very carefully. What Keith – it was usually Keith in current affairs – was talking about was like an adventure story, or a fantasy film, which you pretty well forgot as soon as it was over.

David still had sessions, at his father's insistence and expense, with Caroline Higgins. He was worried about Mr Temple, but decided not to mention it, either to his father or to Caroline. He had worked out what they would say, and was convinced nothing could be achieved by confiding in them.

For convenience, David's sessions with Caroline were going to continue to be conducted at the Hall, rather than his flat. Caroline came in a gleaming 4WD Porsche, which she used to park off the premises, until it was vandalised by local lads from the housing estate. She may have parked off the property at first because her vehicle was so big, or because it looked incongruous beside the battered little bombs driven by the staff. David had seen her arrive on a number of occasions when he had been outside. She had the invariable practice of getting out of the vehicle, shaking her long, straight, blonde hair, and deftly fixing it in a bun at the back of her neck.   And once, as she crossed the path to the door, he saw her slip a diamond ring off her finger, remove the diamond studs from her ears, drop them in her handbag, and wipe off her lip gloss with a tissue. By the time Caroline arrived at the doors of the Hall, she always looked simple and demure.

Caroline had long been troubled by David's connection with Cathy Marsden, and had concerns about how it had affected him. She had seen the prominent coloured photograph in his room, taken at the party, showing Cathy with Poppy beside her, and a pyramid of residents, and staff, gathered around the wheelchair. Cathy looked like an Egyptian princess with her pet lion, and servants.

Caroline thought that his close association with a fiftyish woman, who eventually could not move or speak, was not entirely healthy. She had stressed to him in her low key manner, and quite obliquely, over a long period, the need to cultivate 'healthy' relationships. David inferred that in Caroline's view, any relationship with a resident, and probably most of the staff, was likely to be unhealthy. He asked her what a 'healthy relationship' was.

Caroline replied, "I mean one that is uplifting, energising, even a little inspiring – as well as good fun. A relationship that adds a dimension to you."

"That's my experience with Cathy," David said.

"But Cathy was very ill, with limited, and failing mental powers."

"True… but what has that got to do with it?" he asked.

Caroline paused, watching him. "Yes. All right, David," she had said, backing away from conflict.

"Can't you give me an answer?" he asked.

"Certainly… you must choose your own friends, and some of them may be sick people. I'm only saying it's good to have friends who are normal and well."

When he asked, "How do you tell who is normal and well?" Caroline had given him one of her tranquil, pin-up poses, showing her shining, even teeth, and said they would talk about it another day. But they never did talk about it.

In the session, before he was due to leave the Hall, Caroline had asked, "Can you tell me if you have any feelings about the decision to move Cathy, David?"

"What happened, is what always happens."

"How do you mean?"

He shrugged, and smiled at the obvious. "She had no say."

Caroline gave the smallest frown. She usually never frowned at all. An instant later, her tanned forehead was as smooth as a ceramic glaze. "Poor Cathy couldn't speak."

"She didn't want to go."

"How do you know that, David?"

"She told me."

Caroline rested her long, immaculately oval fingernails on the tabletop in a row and contemplated them. "Are you sure she could tell you?"

"Yes."

"I see. Very well. But you know, the doctors and other people caring for Cathy knew what was best for her."

They were back to the same old thing again. "That's what I said ... that's what always happens."

"Do you feel that's what's happened to you? What always happens?"

"Yes."

"Didn't you have a say?"

"I nearly didn't. If you can't speak much, you don't have a say. Even if you can speak, it sometimes doesn't matter."

There was a long pause while Caroline considered her own involvement. "Are you annoyed with anybody about this?"

"No."

"You're sure?"

"It's the way it goes."

"Good. Do you have any feelings about Cathy, now, that you can tell me about?"

"She's fine."

"David, can you explain that a little more?"

"Well… she's out of her body, which wasn't much use."

"Do you have any feeling about that, her being out of her body?"

"If she had stayed here, the last brick wouldn't have been put in the wall yet … maybe not for a while."

"Which wall is that?"

"The wall around Cathy."

"She had a wall around her? How do you know?"

"She told me."

"Does anybody else know about the wall?"

"I don't think so."

"I see … Can you tell me who put the last brick in the wall?"

"The people caring for Cathy."

"David, I don't want you to let what happened to Cathy upset you. We can talk about it, and you'll see that everybody was trying to do their best for a very sick person."

"I'm not upset… Things happen this way."

"You're sure?"

"I'm fine because Cathy's fine."

Caroline was silent, thinking, and although she did not say it, David could see that what he had said was not acceptable to her.

"David, I'm going to tell your father that we need to go on seeing each other. Agreed?"

David let Caroline take his silence as assent, because it was useful to have a telephone line into another world.

33

David didn't read newspapers, but Keith did, when he was in charge of the day shift, and had to review current affairs. Shortly before David was due to leave Denby Hall, Keith came to his room with a copy of the local paper, *The Enquirer*, in his hand.

"Do you see this, David? About the husband of that snotty bitch in Eccleston Street."

David had a sick feeling. "What's happened?"

He had thought much about his blundering intervention into Mr Temple's life. He remained unhappy with Anita's robust verdict that Graham Temple would soon recover. If it had not looked like interfering, he would have gone to see Mr Temple, but he was afraid that in some way, which he was not clever enough to appreciate, he might provoke another firestorm of emotion. He had, nevertheless, taken to walking Poppy, when Helmut brought her to the Hall, past the Eccleston Street property, half hoping that he might meet Mr Temple casually, and they could talk.

"He's won a prize," Keith said. "Apparently he's a historian. Written a book about Christian missionaries in Japan in the seventeenth century. Now there's a topical subject for you. Quite a learned old geezer…What's the matter?"

"I … met him, that's all."

David liked Keith, but he wasn't the sort of person he could tell about Mr Temple. Nobody knew what had happened except Anita and Desmond.

Later in the day, he made his slow pace to Eccleston Street with Poppy, and stood for a while across the road under the trees, looking at the house. He remembered the plush reception room with the big smoky mirror, the Filipino servant, Poppy galumphing down the hall and, on his last visit, Mr Temple, at first jovial, and then bent over in the chair, in agony.

"What have I done?" he had asked himself a dozen times.

Poppy began to bark, lurching out onto the road in the direction of number 73, and jerking David so hard that his back hurt. Mr Temple was on the doorstep, and he had seen them.

"Ha! The lad that pricked the balloon!" Mr Temple shouted. "And the superb Justina!"

Poppy obviously knew and liked Mr Temple, and she strained hard towards him. David followed willingly. The tone of Mr Temple's shouts was friendly. Mr Temple made a fuss of Poppy, slapping her, rubbing her muzzle, and letting Poppy take his hand in her mouth.

"I've been missing you, old girl!"

"I could bring Poppy – what we call her – round sometimes, if you like," David said, seizing on the one positive contribution he could make.

"But it's Anita's dog. And I don't think I'll be seeing all that much of her, unless it's in a solicitor's office."

"No, Anita and Desmond gave her to Helmut, the boss of Denby Hall."

"I see," Mr Temple said, nonplussed. "Very kind of them."

"I get to walk her a lot and I could bring her round."

"Would you do that?" Mr Temple asked, looking at David as though such a gratuitous offer could not be serious.

"Sure. It's no trouble."

"I'd like that. Really. I'll give you my number. Anyway, come in, come in – David, isn't it? – and bring... Poppy. Let's call her Poppy."

David followed Mr Temple, and Poppy, into the house. The atmosphere of gloom and neglect, which he had imagined, was not apparent. The stereo speakers in the rooms were playing a symphony that he remembered faintly, and could probably once have performed on the piano. Mr Temple saw his attention was drawn to the music.

"You know it? Mozart, 21 in C Major. A delight," he said, whistling a few bars in tune with the pianist.

"I used to play …before my accident."

"Well, have a cup of tea … no danger of being hit by flying vases today, eh? Ha ha!"

Poppy stretched out comfortably on the rug before the fireplace. Mr Temple fussed over the silver tea tray, with its Royal Doulton crockery, which the maid had brought.

"Beautiful stuff, this. Don't you think? I mean, no point in making do with a cafeteria cup when you can experience the exquisite. I'll play mum. I am the mum here now!" he said, pouring into the ornate pink and yellow cups.

Mr Temple's long, silver hair was carefully groomed, and he looked bright and energetic in his smoothly ironed pink shirt. He asked a few courteous questions about David's health, and then cut to a point that was bothering him. His gaze was alert, and much more youthful than his rather slow manner implied.

"Tell me why Poppy has come to Denby Hall."

"She wanted to be there, when Cathy was there."

"Ah, yes … but Mrs Marsden is not there now. Tell me why you've been coming past the house. I've seen you a couple of times before."

"I … was thinking about you."

"Why me?"

"Because I … upset your life."

"Ha! That's very thoughtful of you, but no need. Burden lifted, David. Burden lifted!"

Mr Temple stood, swaying thoughtfully to the music. When he sat down he focussed unblinkingly on David. He asked a lot of questions about how David came into the situation, and what he knew. David didn't feel he was being interrogated, only that he was giving a necessary explanation of his friendship with Cathy and Desmond, and his words flowed easily in the cordial atmosphere.

"Mrs Temple also came to see me to say sorry about the row here," David concluded.

"Quite right too. The least she could do. You seem to have been in the eye of the typhoon."

"I just wanted Cathy to see Poppy."

"What a dominant person she was."

"I don't think she intended that. It's more what people did because of her."

"Anyway, it's good of you to think of me. If it will make things easier for you, I don't mind telling you my side. It's very simple, and no secret. I think we've washed the Temples' grubby linen in the neighbourhood's streets, and hung it out on the trees! We're well known around here. My wife was in public life. Oh yes, I was hurt at first, the victim of long-term deception. How could my wife do this to me? But I simmered down in a matter of hours. I took an honest look at what I have *endured*. Anita and I were two people who found it convenient, for rather warped reasons, to share the same house. And for both us, in that, there was a strain. For Anita it was the tension of deception. For me it was the tension of fitting somebody into my life whom I should have left years ago. I never knew about Marsden, but I did think Anita could have had a lover, or perhaps lovers – this was a direction in which I preferred not to look. I ignored the possibility. I built a kind of mental barrier that cut me off from the possibility. Not much point in complaining when the possibility turns out to be a reality. Now I'm free!"

The music had stopped. Mr Temple, belying his sluggish manner, jumped to his feet. Poppy sprang up too, and whined, and Mr Temple rolled her over on her back, tickling her belly.

"You will bring her round?"

"I will. I'll give you a call," David said, fingering the card Mr Temple handed to him.

"But in the meantime, I'm off to Hawaii to attend a conference, and collect a prize!"

As David moved slowly down Eccleston Street with Poppy, he thought again about Cathy's notion of coupledom. David's worry about the Anita-Graham couple, slitting its own belly in a sad, and bloody seppuku, was wrong. It had, instead, shed the dead husk of its own coupledom, and released two individuals.

And from a creature of the half-light, Desmond-Anita had become a being, with full strength, and enthusiasm for life. David tried to see the tortuous course the reborn creature might follow, as it twisted and turned on the journey – through various homes, and hotels, and trips to Ascot, and holidays on Caribbean islands, its two pairs of eyes glaring out in different directions, its two half-brains, each frantically trying to decipher the confusion of messages from the other half-brain. David felt glad to just have Poppy.

One day, after lunch, Helmut came into the dining room leading Poppy, to everybody's surprise except David's. Helmut had with him Rose, and Ian, who had been promoted from a shift manager, to the new post of manager of Denby Hall. Instead of the usual uniform shirt, Ian wore an old grey suit, dating from a time when he was less muscular. His strong neck stuck out, and his bare wrists protruded from the short sleeves.

Cathy's party aside, it was unheard of and against the rules to bring an animal inside the Hall – although Helmut made the rules. When they saw Poppy, the residents began clapping, whistling, shouting, and stamping their feet. Poppy put her nose in the air, and howled in what seemed an acknowledgement.

"Sit, Poppy, sit!" Helmut commanded, and Poppy obeyed, wriggling her nose, and scraping her wagging tail on the floor. When Poppy did this and she was excited, as she was now, she shifted her weight, lifting one front paw an inch, and then the other, jigging on the spot without changing her position. She exuded enthusiasm that was catching.

Helmut called for order, and the spoon banging eventually stopped.

"I want to tell you today that Poppy is going to have a new master. You will all be able to to see her more often, because   I am giving her to David Thurgood!"

David had already discussed this with Helmut, who knew how much he wanted to look after Poppy. She had become a kind of unofficial mascot of Denby Hall. Helmut had satisfied himself that Poppy could be housed and fed at David's apartment. He had said how difficult it was for him to arrange for Poppy to have a good walk each day, because an increasing amount of his time was spent at the Kent neuro-disability home, where none of the patients could help, because none were mobile, and he was too busy.

David rose from the table, and crossed the floor to thank Helmut, and take Poppy's leash.

Pandemonium broke out – or rather resumed – at the conclusion of Helmut's announcement, and did not end until Keith rushed up and down the main aisle, waving the residents back to their seats, and shouting, "Come on now, fair's fair!" and David led Poppy outside.

Each day, when David was working at Denby Hall, he walked Poppy to the grounds, and tied her to the garden seat on the porch. Residents who were able to come and go, often spent time with her. Those who were well enough, but not allowed out alone, would sometimes gather on the porch with a care assistant, on a fine day, to have a smoke. Poppy was often the centre of this group. Poppy's leash was long enough for her to sit in front of the lobby windows, which she sometimes did when she was alone, looking into the Hall, her head moving from side to side, as she puzzled about the movements of the people behind the glass.